DEFIANT

LIPSTICK AND LEAD BOOK 7

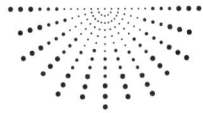

SYLVIA MCDANIEL

VIRTUAL BOOKSELLER, LLC

Copyright
Copyright © 2019 Sylvia McDaniel
Published by Virtual Bookseller, LLC
All Rights Reserved
Cover Design: Dar Albert
Edited by Tina Winograd
Release date: May 2019
ebook ISBN: 978-1-942608-99-8
Paperback ISBN: 978-1-950858-03-3

This book and parts thereof may not be reproduced in any form, stored in a retrieval system, or transmitted in any form by any means—electronic, mechanical, photocopying, or otherwise—without prior written permission of the author and publisher, except as provided by the United States of America copyright law. The only exception is by a reviewer who may quote short excerpts in a review.

O

Some Husbands Just Won't Die

On the brink of losing everything, Dora Tennyson learns her dead husband is alive and well in Fort Worth. And married. Determined to capture the man who stole her inheritance, she becomes a bounty hunter. Only problem is three orphaned children and one gorgeous cowboy stand in her way.

Jesse Moore vows revenge on the man who fatally poisoned his sister—Leo Tennyson…her husband. Raising his sister's three children, he's shocked when a woman shows up claiming to be Leo's legal wife.

Who will find Leo first, the betrayed bounty hunter or the enraged brother? Along the trail, sparks fly between Dora and Jesse, igniting an inferno. Will desire bind them together forever or will a secret Dora keeps tear them apart?

Want to learn about my new releases before anyone else? Sign up for my New Book Alert and receive a free book.

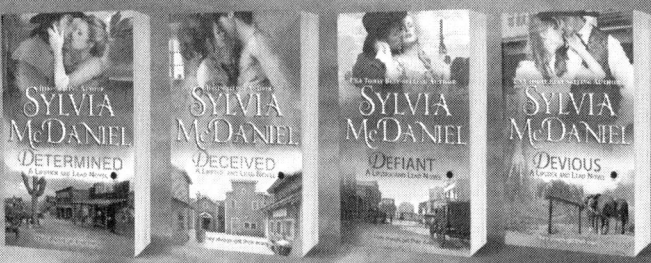

SYLVIA McDANIEL
Lipstick and Lead Series
www.sylviamcdaniel.com

Lipstick and Lead Series

Desperate
Deadly
Dangerous
Daring
Determined
Deceived
Defiant
Devious
Lipstick and Lead Box Set Books 1-4
Lipstick and Lead Box Set Books 5-9
**Quinlan's Quest

CHAPTER ONE

March 1889, Zenith, Texas

"Your dead husband is alive," Sheriff Zach Taylor said, sitting across from Dora Tennyson in her parlor. Through the open window, birds tweeted, calling to one another in the spring sunshine.

Dora jerked back like she'd been slapped. A low buzz built in her ears as all the blood in her body seemed to drain. Her vision slowly darkened, and she feared she would faint. Shaking her head, she stared at the sheriff, disbelief overwhelming her. How could Leo be alive?

"But the telegram from the Dodge City sheriff?" she said, staring at the lawman. "It said he was killed in a shootout."

"Someone might have forged the sheriff's name." With a sigh, Zach shook his head. "In Fort Worth, I was sure I saw him standing on the corner, selling a miracle cure-all drink. No doubt in my mind it was Leo. The moment he saw me, he packed up and left. I searched and couldn't find him."

Oh my, that sounded so like her sneaky husband. At the first sign of trouble, he would fold and run. In their marriage, in business, and evidently, even in card playing. "Why would he lie?"

"Didn't you say he cleaned out your bank account? Could there be another woman?"

Hysterical laughter exploded from Dora. What woman in their right mind would want Leo? She had been crazy to let her father convince her to marry him.

"Greed is his mistress," she said, thinking about the day she learned all their money was gone except a small amount. Right there in the middle of the bank, she fainted and dropped to the floor like a bullet hit her. Now, now, she would find that lousy, no-good thief. Now, she would...do what?

"You think he's living in Fort Worth?" she asked.

"Don't rightly know," he said. "Wouldn't hurt to look. Maybe he's still out on a street corner, selling over glorified tonic that's nothing more than flavored water."

A laugh escaped from her tight chest. Leo had found a new con game. What had he done with her inheritance?

Just when her finances forced her to take a husband, she learned she was no longer a widow, only broke.

A fire ignited inside her, spreading through her body like a wildfire out of control. Tired of being a victim of her husband and unwilling to accept his schemes any longer, she spoke aloud, "I'm going to find that cheating thief, and this time, this time, he will most definitely need an undertaker. This time, I'll damn sure be a widow. This time, he won't rise from the dead."

"Now, Dora, all you know is that he faked his death and stole your money. Maybe he had a reason for his actions," the sheriff said. She knew he was only trying to calm her. She would have none of it, because she was done being taken advantage of by her dead husband.

The sheriff continued, "I'm your friend, Dora, but also a lawman. Don't want to hear you threatening to kill him in front of me."

"What would you do in my situation?"

Conflicted, the sheriff sat in the best chair in her parlor without saying a word.

Too roused to heed her friend's warning, she said, "Oh, he's a dead man selling a miracle drink he's going to need." She stared into the sheriff's green eyes. "If he had a valid reason, he should have explained why to his wife. Instead, he lied, and for five long years, I believed I was a widow."

"Dora, you're in shock."

Maybe so, but that didn't matter.

After waiting years, she made the decision to find an older man of means to marry. Now, almost penniless, even that option was gone. The new dress she ordered that was to be her courting gown would be ready today.

A perfectly timed joke. Now, instead, the beautiful material would be her catch-her-dead-husband outfit.

"I'm going after him," she said, her resolve strengthening. "Leo Tennyson is going to give me my money back. Then I'm going to kill him."

CHAPTER TWO

Dora had lived in Zenith the last ten years, but until recently, she'd never met the McKenzie girls. Now standing in Meg's dress shop while she finished pinning up her skirt, she realized they were the answer to her dilemma. For the last half hour, she listened to the women congratulating Caroline for bringing in bounties.

Desperate for money, after listening to these strong ladies, she saw an opportunity to fix her cash flow. If she became a bounty hunter, she could apprehend her lying husband and possibly even collect a reward on the bastard.

And if he didn't return her inheritance, then at least she would have a skill to earn money chasing outlaws and criminals. Now the way she felt, the man was a dead man as far as she was concerned. For five years, she'd lived with guilt, thinking she was glad Leo was dead, only to learn the rotten scoundrel still walked the earth.

But not for long. Still, how would she find him?

The women seemed to be winding down after their lengthy conversation on Caroline's new man. The man wrote fiction and he'd written a story about Caroline that didn't put her in a favorable light. In retaliation, Caroline scribbled across his script he was a horrible lover.

Still, Dora had some business she needed to discuss.

Meg glanced at Caroline. "I'm concerned about something you said. Was he a lousy lover?"

Caroline blushed, her cheeks rosy. "No, he was excellent, but I knew those hurtful words would help him understand my pain."

The ladies laughed and sighed. "Thank goodness," Meg said.

Waiting on the raised platform, Dora cleared her throat to get their attention.

"Oh no, I'm so sorry, Mrs. Tennyson. In all the drama, I completely forgot you were standing there."

Dora didn't mind, the time had given her a chance to learn more about the women. Quickly, she came to some conclusions.

"Not a problem. What an interesting conversation. Now, I have a proposition. I'd like to enroll in your bounty hunting school. After almost ten years, I have a score to settle."

Meg stepped over to the woman. "Why do you want to join our program? You realize what you're getting into, right? You'll be taught how to ride a horse, follow tracks, read wanted posters, and more importantly, how to handle a gun. We'll teach you everything you need to know to become a successful bounty hunter."

This was exactly what she needed. Afterward, she could make a decent living and not have to depend on a man or reveal her deepest, darkest secret.

Laughter escaped Dora. "That's what I need. My dead husband has come back to life and I intend to make certain he remains dead after I get my money back."

Ruby shook her head. "I don't know. Our school does not produce killers. We teach women a skill that will help them earn a living."

At least this expertise would not include going to work for a saloon and becoming a whore. The only person she wanted to kill was Leo. Everyone else, she simply would arrest and bring to justice. But after Leo put her in this tenuous position, he deserved to die.

With a sigh, Dora glanced at her. "In about ninety days, my cash will run out. This dress I purchased with the idea of enticing an older man to court and eventually marry me. But now I'm still a married woman, so remarrying is out. Becoming a bounty hunter sounds like a wonderful plan. Even if I find Leo, I still will need a way to make money that doesn't involve me lying on my back."

The women nodded. "She's got a point," Caroline said. "Money just doesn't fall out of the sky. Bounty hunting is not easy. So if you're not into hard work and long days, then that job of lying on your back might be more for you."

The woman belonged in a crazy home if she thought she would become a whore. "No."

"We start on Monday," Ruby said. "Bring your own pistol. Preferably a Colt forty-five."

"Welcome to the club," Meg said.

"Oh hell, another one," Annabelle said with a smile. "Welcome."

Dora grinned, and for the first time in weeks, peace came over her. Maybe she wouldn't starve after all.

CHAPTER THREE

Two months later, Dora felt ready to hunt and face her dead husband. After going on a raid to save Quinlan Adams, she was confident in her abilities to fire a gun and angry enough no one better mess with her.

After all, this would be her new occupation. Her livelihood would keep her from going hungry. And she would soon get her revenge.

Addie King, another student at the school, came up to her. "There's a telegram waiting for you. Do you think it's from that investigator you hired?"

A tremor of excitement filled her. After selling her home, she took some of the money and employed a man to find Leo. What if he'd located her once-dead husband? Then she could begin her journey.

A tiny spiral of fear zipped through her, but she refused to acknowledge the emotion. No matter what, she would always show only strength on the outside. She might be terrified on the inside, but externally she would appear like a mean woman carrying a gun. Someone you didn't mess with.

"Guess, I better go find out. What are you going to do?"

"Target practice. See that can sitting on the fence? That's for my brother. The second can is for my sister. And the third, my mother."

All of her family had been killed in a raid on their farm. A mistaken-identity attack that left them dead. Addie had gone to the outhouse, which none of the outlaws checked, where she watched the entire invasion on their farm.

The house and barn burned to the ground, but the outhouse stood. Now she wanted revenge, though she never mentioned her intentions to Ruby.

Dora reached out and touched Addie on the arm. "Kill those cans."

"Thanks," she said. "I think I will."

With hurried steps, Dora almost ran to the house where Ruby's office was. The poor woman's pregnancy was beginning to really swell her body and a twinge of jealousy filled Dora.

At the very least, Leo could have given her children. For five years, they had tried, and she never became pregnant. Maybe being childless was for the best. But a child would have given her a reason to continue to live on. Now she had nothing but her need for revenge.

As she walked into the house, she all but ran into Ruby. "No surprise to see you here. You must have heard about the telegram."

For the last two months, Dora had resided at Ruby and Deke's home. The couple were so cute together, but Dora witnessed the fear in Deke's eyes. His first wife died from childbirth and he was frightened for Ruby who kept reassuring him she would be fine. Dora had confidence Ruby would be. Because she was a strong, determined woman.

"Is the telegram from the investigator?" she asked.

"Don't know," Ruby said and handed her the paper. "Deke brought the missive from town and we haven't read it."

With trembling hands, Dora glanced at the words. "That son

of a bitch. He married a woman and bought land with my money in Grayson County, near Gainesville."

Ruby didn't say anything but stared at her.

"Do you think I'm ready?" Dora asked.

The woman she'd become good friends with smiled. "Of course. You helped rescue Quinlan, didn't you? I've seen you hit a target without looking. We taught you how to build a fire, hide, read tracks. Now is your first test. My only concern is your hate for this man. Remember, you do not have the right to kill someone."

No, but she would make him hurt really bad and it could be self-defense.

"Understand," Dora said. "More than anyone, you know how much I want to find him."

"Yes, I do," she said. "Take enough rations for at least two weeks. To reach Gainesville will take you five hard days of traveling. Don't trust strangers along the road. When you arrive, you might want to talk to the sheriff and tell him your intentions."

Dora would stop at the sheriff's office only long enough to learn if Leo had a price on his head. Other than that, she would go directly to this ranch he bought in Gainesville. If he purchased the land with her money, his new wife would have the shock of her life when Dora took possession and sold the place.

"Oh, you think he'll let me string him up?"

Ruby laughed. "I'm going to worry about you. Don't be my first trained killer."

With a sigh, Dora accepted it would be difficult to kill Leo, anyone else next to impossible.

Reaching out, she took Ruby's hand. "Never would I murder him in cold blood, but I would be lying to you if I said he'll be alive when this is over. Right now, you should worry about this baby and your husband. Thanks for helping and teaching me so much. In the morning when I leave, I'm confidant Leo will soon be looking out of a jail cell."

Or even better, a coffin.

"Thank you for saying jail cell and not coffin," Ruby said with a smile.

Thankfully, the woman couldn't read her thoughts.

"You're welcome, Dora. Now let's hope Addie will soon be ready to go on her journey."

A frown crossed Dora's face. Had Ruby learned of Addie's past? When she walked out the door, she let Addie's problems go. There was enough going on in her life that she couldn't stick her nose in Addie's business.

CHAPTER FOUR

On a ranch in north Texas, Jesse Moore sat in a chair at his sister's bedside, watching her struggle to breath. The illness, whatever it was, had come upon her swiftly. This morning, he went for the doctor, but the man didn't give him much hope.

Day before yesterday, she'd been fine, but last night he awoke to the sounds of her retching. When she didn't rise from bed this morning, he checked on her to discover her eyes were yellow, her breathing shallow. Immediately, he rode for the doctor and insisted the man come examine her.

His eight-year-old niece, Grace, fed her little sister, Ella, and even younger brother, eighteen-month-old Ben. Not certain what had befallen their mother, she kept them occupied in the other room. Every time Jesse stepped out, her worried gaze followed him.

His worthless brother-in-law was off peddling some medical miracle cure and had left his sister here to care for the ranch and the children. On a routine visit, he came out to install the cabinets he made for Ida and now she lay here in bed dying.

What if he hadn't been here? Grace was a smart, mature kid, but she was still a child. Damn Leo for not staying home.

"Jesse," Ida said, her eyes beseeching. "Promise me you will take care of my babies. Leo...he's not responsible. Don't let him have them or they will suffer."

At the thought of her dying, his heart clenched with pain. When their parents died over ten years ago, he'd raised fifteen-year-old Ida. Now she lay on her death bed asking him to become the guardian of her kids.

Why did it feel like he'd been watching over and taking care of Ida her entire life and now she was giving him a huge responsibility?

More than anything, he didn't want her to die. Those babies needed their mother, not their uncle.

"No, you're going to be fine," he said, picking up her hand, wanting so badly to believe she would recover.

"Promise me," she said.

With a sigh, he closed his eyes trying to keep the tears that clogged his throat from spilling down his cheeks. He opened his eyes and stared down at his sister, her body a sickly shade of blue.

"You know I love the children and I'll do whatever I can for them, but they need you. Grace is going to be a young woman soon. She needs her mother."

How could he raise two young girls and a baby? This was more than he could handle, and yet he couldn't say no.

"There is money hidden in a jar in the back of the cellar. Take the cash. Put the land in the children's names. That way their father can't sell the land and run. Ben is going to be the one most affected by this. Grace can help you."

Gasping for air, she paused and caught her breath, then continued on like she only had moments to tell him everything he needed to know. "Poor Ella is going to be shaken. Because she's nervous, she needs more attention. Grace is my rock, my helper, and she'll hide her emotions of how this is affecting her."

Ida took a deep breath. "Bring them to me. I don't have long."

Her words shook him, and he released her hand. Turning from her, he wiped his eyes and tried to put on a brave face, knowing this would be the hardest day of his life, watching his nieces and nephew say goodbye to their mother. Clearing his throat, he tried to appear calm as he stepped to the door of the bedroom.

"Grace, you and the kids come in here."

His niece came around the corner, holding little Ben, her eyes wide with fright. "Is it Momma?"

The girl was too smart for her age.

"Bring your brother and sister and come in here. Your mother wants to talk to you," he said, his voice strained.

Like she was walking to face a firing squad, Grace stepped toward him, her hand reached out and clasped Ella's in hers as she entered her mother's room. As they approached the bed, Jesse hung back.

Ida tried to smile, but he could see her strength ebbing.

"My babies," she said, a tear escaping her eye. "Life is hard and sometimes you are called home before you're ready to go. Grace, the others will never remember this day, but you tell them how I loved you and didn't want to leave, but I have no choice. Uncle Jesse is going to take care of you."

She coughed and it took her a moment to recover. "Always know that I love you and I'll be watching over you, protecting you, and wishing I was with you."

"Momma, please don't die," Grace said, her voice choking as tears escaped down her cheeks. "Please."

Reaching out, Ida stroked her face. "God is calling me home. Be strong for your brother and sister. Take--care of them--for me. I love you."

Jesse could see his sister struggled to say those last words.

With despair, he watched as Ida glanced at him and smiled, looked at her children one more time before her eyes closed and she gasped, the air leaving her lungs.

Pain gripped his chest as he wrapped his arms around his nieces and nephew, tears flowing down his cheeks. Their mother was gone and now their care was up to him. What was a bachelor going to do with three children?

And where the hell was his worthless brother-in-law?

CHAPTER FIVE

Dora rode her tan mare onto what she hoped was the Tennyson Farm. Gazing around, she wondered where Leo was hiding. If he'd seen her, he would have hightailed it out of here.

Instead, she saw a young girl with a basket in the hen house and a little girl about five chasing after a baby who squealed with delight as he ran from her. A garden was over to the side of a small house with a big porch that circled the front and sides. The shaded veranda looked like the perfect place to enjoy tea in the afternoon or sit outside and read a book.

Out in the fields, a man walked behind a plow, but from his rock-hard body she could tell he wasn't Leo. A large hat covered his head, but his muscular arms and long legs were nothing like her dead husband's physique.

"Ma'am, are you lost?" a little girl, the one who had been gathering eggs, asked.

Green eyes stared up at Dora, the child's reddish-brown hair was pulled back in a ponytail. One day the child would be a beauty, but for now, she was curious about a woman sitting a horse in a split skirt. Meg had given Dora one of her famous riding skirts. And it was a lifesaver.

"No, I'm looking for Leo Tennyson. Have you seen him?"

The girl who appeared to be about eight frowned at her. "He's not here."

Just then the man walked toward them, and the closer he came, the more Dora's chest seemed to tighten. The heat from the summer sun had him sweating, taking out a handkerchief and swiping the moisture from his brow. The urge to garner more information from this girl before the man arrived had her gazing down at the child.

"Do you know where he is?"

"No, ma'am," she said, not giving away any additional news.

For some reason, Dora felt this child knew more than she was telling. Now the man stood in front of her staring up at her with the most beautiful deep brown eyes and lashes. Her breath caught in her throat at his looks.

"Can I help you?"

"Looking for Leo Tennyson," she said.

The man laughed. "He's not home."

The baby yanked off his diaper and went running through the yard with the younger girl chasing him.

"Ben, come back here. I need to change you."

The little boy giggled, racing as fast as his short, fat legs would carry him toward the man.

"Ella," the older girl said. "Put a diaper on him."

"I'm trying," the young girl said.

The man reached down and scooped the naked baby up into his arms. The sight of the man holding his bare-bottom son caused Dora's chest to constrict. A man who cared about children, what an anomaly. How fortunate for his wife.

"Little man, you're being ornery today. Stop giving your sister so much trouble and let her put a diaper on."

"There's no clean ones," Ella, the little girl said. "And he refuses to wear the wet one."

"This morning, I washed a load. They are hanging outside on the line. Go back there and get one."

For a moment, Dora's heart contracted. How neat to have a house full of children running around, depending on you to care for them. Yet the sight only made her ache for what she could never have. Shaking her head, she tried to bring the conversation back to Leo.

"So Leo lives here," she said.

The man frowned. "Yes, he's out selling his wares. We don't know when he'll return."

She nodded thinking this couldn't be good. "Do you have any idea where he went?"

"Lady, if I knew where he went, I'd be going after him and dragging him home. His children need him," he said, gazing at her, the barely concealed anger coming through in his voice. A buzzing noise began in her brain.

A gasp escaped from her, leaving her reeling. "*His* children?"

The man looked at her like she'd lost her mind. "Yes, the two younger kids are his."

Dora couldn't stop her reaction. Like someone struck her, the blow to her heart left her shuddering. The son of a bitch had children, yet they never had babies.

Which meant all along, the problem was she had been barren and not him. Now was not the time, so she shoved aside the thought. Right now, she couldn't deal with this realization.

Pain clenched her chest and she tried her best to stop thinking about the consequences of what she had learned. Staring at the children, tears welled up in her eyes and she quickly swallowed.

"Is he married?" she finally asked.

The man frowned. "Leo was married to my sister Ida. Unfortunately, she passed away almost a month ago. Haven't seen him in probably going on two months."

At the thought of these children not having a mother, her hand went to her chest and she sighed. "I'm so sorry."

He handed the naked baby to Ella. "Grace is getting a diaper. Take him into the house and make certain he has clothes on before he comes outside again."

After the child walked away, he turned his attention back to her. "Frankly, she's better off."

The man would never hear a disagreement from her as she watched his two children walking toward the house, her heart breaking.

"Who are you?" he asked. "Why are you asking all these questions?"

With them now alone, she could tell him the truth. Though she would have liked to keep that information to herself for a little while longer. But he asked and deserved to understand what kind of person his brother-in-law truly was.

"My name is Dora Tennyson. I'm his wife."

CHAPTER SIX

*J*esse gazed at the woman sitting on her horse in the yard, proclaiming to be Leo's wife. "Mrs. Tennyson, I'm Jesse Moore, by the way. Why don't you come sit a spell on the porch and drink a glass of tea?"

She smiled at him. "Please call me Dora."

"That might be wise, especially because of the children," he said. "After all, you share the same last name."

Dora swung her leg over the saddle and dropped to the ground like she'd been riding all her life. Leading the horse to the hitching post in the front of the house, she tied the reins and followed him up the steps.

Curious, Grace came back outside with Ben and Ella in tow.

This would be an adult conversation that needed privacy. Jesse looked at Grace. "Why don't you take the kids inside and give them a snack? Me and Mrs. Dora are going to sit out here and talk."

"Yes, sir," Grace said, her green eyes flashing with anger. Life had dealt this kid so much heartache, she didn't deserve to hear how her other parent was such a low life.

The two of them went into the shade, taking the two chairs from the porch. "Would you like something to drink?"

"No, I'm fine," she said.

"You wed Leo?" he asked, staring at her.

The laugh that resounded from her sounded hollow. "Ten years ago. Until a couple months ago, I believed I was a widow."

That was hard to comprehend. How could the woman believe her husband was dead and suddenly learn he still lived? Didn't make a bit of sense, but then again, what about Leo ever made sense? A careless individual. Leo's interests were only what pleased him at the moment, including women.

Not knowing someone was alive was a stretch of Jesse's imagination.

"At eighteen, I married Leo in Fort Worth at the county courthouse. For years, we struggled. After my father died, I collected a small inheritance."

In the shadows, he watched her take a deep relaxing breath.

"Not too long after the money was deposited, Leo took off on a business trip to Dodge City, Kansas. About two weeks after he left, I received a telegram from the sheriff telling me he had been killed in a shootout. So I went down to the bank and behold, the account with my inheritance had been cleaned out. Since then, I've lived off our meager savings, which I think he forgot about."

Leaning back in the chair, she gazed at the land. "Looks like my money bought a nice place."

His sister's voice telling him to put the land in the children's names startled him. Why had he not gone to the courthouse and changed the title before now? The property was in Leo's name and if what she said was true, the children would have nothing. "I don't know if he bought this place or my sister did."

"Did he marry Ida?"

Oh, how Jesse didn't want to answer her question, but what good would it do to lie to the woman. Very easily the record of their marriage could be located at the Grayson County courthouse. "Yes, they married about five years ago. Ella and Ben came along soon after."

A funny expression crossed her face, a grimace of what looked like pain. One he didn't understand. This wasn't the first time he mentioned Leo's children. Yet she never said how many kids she and Leo had together.

"Were you happy being married to Leo?"

Her shoulders rose in a shrug. "Not really. Often times, I fussed at him for not having a consistent job. Leo always searched for the fast, easy, money, nothing steady."

Jesse thought of his brother-in-law and knew what she said was true. Right now, Leo was off selling some miracle cure that would make them thousands. But if Dora married him first, Leo had broken the law.

"How could he have wed you and Ida at the same time? That's bigamy."

A chuckle escaped her, and she gazed at him. "Who is going to catch him? Who is going to question if a man had multiple wives?"

She had a point. There were no marriage lawmen saying *wait a minute, you're married*. How would anyone know? At least his sister would never learn her wedding had been illegal.

And when he found his brother-in-law, no other woman would need to worry about him marrying again, because he would have no use for a woman. The man had done this to two women. What if more were tied to Leo?

"Are you sure you're the only one he married?" Jesse asked. "If he did this to you and my sister, what if there are others?"

A frown furrowed Dora's brow and the urge to reach up and soothe the wrinkle overwhelmed him. A gorgeous woman with her blonde hair and soft blue eyes and yet she showed no fear. In fact, she almost seemed like a warrior the way she rode in here and stood up to him.

"It's possible there are more victims of Leo," she said. "Never thought about how many he might have married. To be honest, I was shocked to learn about the farm. Didn't know about the children. I'm sorry if I upset them."

"Yeah, they've had a rough time with their mother dying so unexpectedly. One day she was fine, and the next day, she was so ill and died not long after that. All I could think about was, what if I hadn't been here? What if she died and left these children alone? Certainly, their father would never be located in an emergency."

The blonde slipped her long hair back over her shoulder. "Have you searched for him?"

"No, been too busy taking care of the kids and hoping he would ride back in here. Now I just want to kill him," Jesse said, knowing it was best that Leo was not around.

The baby came running out the door with the other two girls chasing after him. "Stop him."

This time the child wore clothes, but in his hands, he held his sister's favorite doll. Reaching down, Jesse scooped him up and sat him on his lap. "Are you tormenting your sister by taking her doll?"

The little boy grinned. "Momma," he asked, looking around the yard.

Every time he said *momma*, Jesse ached with the loss of his sister. Ida should've been alive and loving them, watching them grow. Ben was still searching for her.

Grace walked out the door and took him from Jesse. Sometimes Grace forgot how to be a child and acted more like an adult.

"Bad," she said, taking the doll from Ben who smiled.

"I should get going and let you get back to work," she said, standing. "Thanks for the information."

The man reached out and touched her arm. "Where are you staying?"

Why did he feel like there was still so much they needed to

discuss? As the hour grew later, he realized it was time to feed and bathe the kids, but he wanted her to stay. No, her spending the night probably wouldn't be considered proper, but three chaperones and the Colt forty-five she wore low on her hips would serve as a deterrent.

"Out on the trail," she said in a rush.

A woman sleeping alone along the road at night? The outlaws, the critters, the snakes all seemed dangerous, but from looking at her, he knew she could take care of herself. Still, he needed to talk more with her and see how much he could learn about Leo.

"Stay here tonight, with me and the kids. We could use the company. You can bunk in my sister's room. Don't worry, we burned the mattress and I put a new one on the bed, thinking I'd sleep in her room, but I couldn't."

"All right," she said. "Only if you let me help you with dinner."

Relief sagged his shoulders. "That would be wonderful."

One night of someone helping him care for these children would be so great. Even if she just helped with the dishes, it would be better than nothing at all. While he loved these kiddos dearly, they were a lot of work.

Odd she didn't offer to help with the children, but that was all right. Just talking to an adult instead of a child would be wonderful. A fabulous experience he wanted so badly.

CHAPTER SEVEN

*A*fter dinner, Dora helped clean up, but Grace acted cold and standoffish and didn't appear to want any help in cleaning the kitchen. Jesse dried the dishes while Grace washed and Dora kept the small children occupied. Poor little Ella seemed almost eager for a woman's touch. The little girl came over and sat in her lap.

"Why are you looking for my papa?" the child asked her, face earnest as she stared at Dora with her large brown eyes.

How did she answer this question and how could she consider killing Leo when he was all these poor children had left for a parent? Now that their mother was dead, maybe she should walk away and let things go on like they were.

What if Jesse lied? Or what if Leo wasn't their father? Had she learned the truth? Yet this situation felt like something Leo would do. Marry an innocent woman and ignore the fact he was already married.

"Your papa and I have some business to discuss," she said, wanting to be honest with this child.

"Did you want to talk with my momma?" she asked and then

solemnly said, "You can't speak to her. She's in heaven. The angels came and took her, even though she didn't want to leave us."

A piece of Dora's heart cracked open, causing her to ache at the loss in this child's voice. A five-year-old shouldn't have been dealing with the death of her mother.

"Yes, your uncle Jesse told me she went to heaven. I would've loved to have met her. I bet she was a great momma to you and a nice lady," she said.

The woman had married her husband, and yet, Dora would never talk badly about her because Ida was a victim as well.

"The best momma ever," Ella said. "Do you have children?"

How did she answer this? People assumed that when you didn't have kids, you didn't like them, when the opposite was true.

"No babies for me," she said, the sadness overwhelming her. After today, she had to face the reality that the problem had not been Leo, but her. Her womb was as barren as the desert and no man would ever want to marry her.

"You could be our new momma," Ella said, smiling at her like she had just thought of the most amazing idea. "Our uncle Jesse, he needs a wife and we need a momma."

Not knowing how to answer, she glanced up and noticed Jesse standing there grinning at her. "Ella, don't scare the woman off. Why don't you get ready for bed? Grace will help you."

Grace stood beside him in the doorway frowning at her sister. The warning glare she shot Dora surprised her. For some reason, the girl hated Dora and she didn't understand why.

"Come on, Ella," she demanded.

Grace sounded more like she was eight going on twenty. The thought of the responsibility bearing down on that child made Dora sad. When she should be playing with dolls, she was taking care of her brother and sister.

Ella gazed at Dora and smiled. "It was nice talking to you."

Glancing at her uncle, she giggled, then leaned into and whispered to Dora, "He needs a wife, real bad. His cooking is lousy."

Laughter bubbled up inside her as the little girl walked over and took her older sister's hand. Skipping down the hall, she waved goodbye as she went toward her bedroom.

"It's been really hard for her since she lost her mother," Jesse said, coming over and sinking into a chair across from Dora. The man had cleaned up before supper and she smelled his clean masculine scent.

The baby crawled up in his lap and he bounced the boy.

"This little guy has shown his displeasure by being more ornery than ever. One moment, he's throwing a temper tantrum, and the next, he's taking his sister's doll and hiding it or crawling up on the counters and getting into trouble. Once I found him wandering in the field. He'd gone in search of his mother."

Jesse hugged the child tightly and the little boy laid his head against his shoulder. Dora's heart cracked. That boy should have been hers and Leo's. Ella should be their child, but instead, Leo had a family with a woman who could give him babies. For a moment, her throat constricted as she swallowed her unshed tears, trying to hide her pain deep inside.

"It's not easy for me to understand why the good Lord thought that Ida had to die. Why didn't he take Leo instead? He's never around. These kids need their mother," Jesse said, gazing down as Ben began to grow sleepy.

His words made Dora sad and she didn't know how to respond. Her mind screaming these children belonged to her and yet they didn't. With a calming breath, she said, "They're lucky they have you."

"Yeah, one of Ida's last request was their father never be allowed to keep the kids. Ida didn't trust him to care for them the way they need."

"Leo didn't tell you what cities he would be traveling to?"

All she wanted was to find Leo and put an end to his miserable life. But what about his family? If she killed Leo, they would be without a father and mother.

A quick glance at her, Jesse's gaze met hers. "Believe me, if I knew where he was, especially after you showed up, I'd go after him and make certain he never harmed anyone else again. No, he doesn't even know his w--my sister is dead."

She thought about where Leo had last been seen. "The sheriff of Zenith saw him selling his miracle cure in Fort Worth. That's how I learned he was still alive. So I hired a private investigator who located the farm."

"You're going to take the farm back, aren't you?"

How could she answer that question? How could she put these children out with no place to go? Right now, the future was unknown, her focus on finding Leo.

"No decision has been made yet, since I don't know what I'm going to do. My inheritance paid for this place, and well, I'm kind of broke at the moment. In fact, I went to bounty hunting school just to be able to track down Leo. Once I locate him, if I don't find my money, I will be forced to become a full-time bounty hunter."

A smile crossed his face. "A woman bounty hunter?"

Why did men consider it such an anomaly for a woman to do a man's job? For years, women stepped in and took over when needed.

"Ever heard of the Lipstick and Lead ladies? Ruby McKenzie -- now Culver and very pregnant--taught me."

"Yes, I have heard of them. Ruby caught the man who killed their father."

"Yes, she did," Dora said, thinking of the women she met who had chosen bounty hunting over being a saloon whore or any other measly job that paid very little.

She stared at this handsome man in front of her. How many men would take on the care of three children? One of whom was just a toddler. "What about you? When you're not caring for your sister's children, what do you do?"

He glanced down at the sleeping baby in his arms, his face tight like he couldn't remember his life before his sister's death. "I'm a carpenter. The reason I was here was to finish the cabinets I built for Ida. Still can't believe she's gone and I'm responsible for her children."

Staring down into the baby's face, he shook his head. "After our parents died, I raised Ida until she turned sixteen, then she married Joe. He was killed when he was thrown from a horse and Grace was two years old. After that, Ida met and wed Leo and two more children came along."

Though his sister was gone, jealousy gripped Dora in a tight hold. The woman had carried not one, but three children, two were Leo's. Sadness seeped from her pores and she sighed knowing she needed to go to her room. The day overwhelmed her, and she longed for private time to let her tears flow.

Rocking the child, Jesse sighed, "After I finished her cabinets, my plan was to head down to the coast and spend some time fishing and relaxing."

"I'm sorry," Dora said. "Doesn't seem fair, but these children would be so lost without you."

"Yes," he said, his voice gruff. "As much as I'd like to go, I can't. They're more important right now."

How did he feel about Leo? What would he do when his brother-in-law returned?

"What about Leo?"

"That son of a bitch better not come back or he's dead. After everything he's put my family through, he's going to die."

Dora sighed. "Not if I find him first."

No way had she come all this distance just to let Leo realize she knew he was still alive. If she saw him, she wanted her money and to tell him the law would be after his lying, cheating ass.

A smile slowly spread across his face. "May the best shooter locate him and finish off his days on this earth."

"And that would be me," she said, rising. "Goodnight, Jesse. I'll be leaving in the morning to locate Leo. Don't worry, I'm going to get to him first."

CHAPTER EIGHT

The next morning, Dora woke coughing, her head pounding with a headache and generally felt lousy. The nights of sleeping outside had finally caught up with her and she feared a bad cold could be coming on. Rising, she dressed and found her way to the kitchen where Jesse cooked breakfast.

"You don't look good," he said, his face turning red as he blushed. "I'm sorry. It's just you're so beautiful and I can see in your eyes, you're not feeling well."

The rugged cowboy was so cute when he became all flustered. Unfortunately, her body ached from the restless nights, waking at every sound in the woods.

"Too many nights sleeping in the night air," she said, coughing. "I should go. Don't want to expose the children and then you really would have your hands full."

If one of these kids became sick because of her, she would be so upset. The man struggled to keep the house running and his family cared for, he didn't need an illness spreading.

Gazing at her, he shook his head. "Nonsense. Rest for a while."

"You need papa's medical cure. I'll go get you a bottle."

Dora frowned. This morning she awoke to a queasy stomach and she wasn't going to drink some rotgut Leo sold to make money. The little girl came up the stairs from the cellar and handed her a glass jar.

"Momma drank a cup full every night and said the miracle cure made her better."

She opened the bottle and poured Dora a drink. Not wanting to hurt the child's feelings, she put the cup up to her lips and pretended to sip. The liquid barely touched her mouth, but the taste was horrible. Ella skipped out of the room, and Dora ran to the open window and tossed the vile stuff out.

Why would anyone drink that concoction?

Jesse stared at her laughing. "That bad?"

"Awful." An involuntary shudder rippled through her. "All I need is some coffee and I'll be on my way."

Jesse poured her a cup of the black stuff and returned to the stove. "Let me fix you some eggs. Besides, I want to talk to you some more about Leo."

Hadn't they discussed everything about her scandalous husband last night? What else did the man need to know?

"What about Leo?" she asked.

When he cracked an egg in the frying pan, the smell sent her stomach revolting. Licking her lips, she tried to rinse the vile drink out of her mouth. Taking a big gulp of coffee, the miracle cure remained on her tongue and a tingle in her lips let her know they were going numb.

"If he was last seen in Fort Worth, it would make sense for him to head to Dallas and down south to the larger towns. He's selling the drink you just had," he said. "He made up about ten batches of the stuff before he left. Ida told me he had the wagon loaded and he wouldn't be home until he sold everything."

Setting the plate of eggs in front of Dora, he sat across from her and she tried not to let the nausea overwhelm her. The man was doing his best to cook for her. Putting a fork full of the breakfast to her lips, she took a bite. The food was delicious, but her intestines began to cramp.

While she concentrated on what he was saying, thinking this made perfect sense and she needed to remember everything, all she wanted to do was lie down. Suddenly her stomach went into full revolt.

Jumping up from the table, she ran out the door and threw up. Leaning against the post, she heaved while he brought her a warm washcloth.

"Maybe you should go back to bed for a while," he said. "You're worse than you're letting on."

With a sigh, she knew she couldn't ride a horse with cramping like this. In fact, the pain was getting worse by the minute.

"Thank you," she said. "Let me just lie down."

What was wrong with her? This morning she could tell a cold was coming on, but now, she had never experienced anything like this. Never. The only thing that could have upset her stomach was that stupid tonic she sipped.

Slowly she made her way back into the house. Pulling off her boots, she laid back on the quilt until the next spasm hit.

What had Ida died from? She forgot to ask.

CHAPTER NINE

Dora's cold suddenly exploded into symptoms that resembled his sisters. Could there be something contagious in the room she picked up? But he and the children had all been in there and none of them were sick. Only his sister and now Dora. What did the two women have in common.

The memory of Ida drinking the miracle tonic she helped Leo create came to mind. The realization that both women drank the juice slammed into Jesse. A sickening sense of unease gripped his chest as he started toward the cellar.

Grace stepped in front of him, her forehead drawn together. "Is that woman sick?"

"Yes."

"What if she makes us all ill?" Grace said. "What if she dies in there just like Momma?"

The kid was smart. Way smarter than him and yet he needed to calm her fears.

"It's not the room, Grace. If it was a germ, we would all be sick," he said, licking his lips wondering if he should be completely honest with the girl. Maybe she knew something about the miracle cure.

"This morning, Ella gave Dora some of your father's miracle tonic. Your mother drank that stuff. Can you show me where they made it?"

His niece's beautiful sapphire eyes widened. "Everything is in the cellar. Momma told me that she and papa had a hard time finding the mushrooms."

"Did she say what kind of mushrooms," he asked, fearing they accidentally found a poisonous mushroom and that's what killed his sister.

The little girl shook her head. "No, let me show you where Momma's been making it for years, but Papa wanted to get on the road, so he made the last couple of batches."

Jesse trusted Ida, she had used herbs and made homemade remedies all her life, but his brother-in-law...Disgust gripped him, holding him hostage.

The man had never been his brother-in-law. Because they weren't legally married. Leo didn't have the brains to create a safe drink to sell to people. Did the miracle cure accidentally kill Ida? Had Leo murdered her with his poisonous concoction?

Grace led the way into the cellar where he lit a lantern. Glancing around the darkened room, he gazed at his sister's supplies. Bottles of carefully labeled herbs lined the wall. Several he noticed bore a skull and crossbones and realized those were poison.

Then he saw the bottle of dried mushrooms. When he picked up the small glass container, he lifted the lid and held it under his nose.

The scent was off—-a strong ammonia smell, rather than the musty odor normally associated with edible plants. What if they harvested the wrong kind? How could he tell?

As he gazed at her herbs, he found a container of charcoal.

"Momma gives us charcoal when we have a tummy ache," Grace said, as she looked around the room. "She promised to teach me about the different plants and how they help you."

The child missed her mother and Jesse realized he could never teach her the knowledge her mother possessed. Right now, he was just doing well to keep everyone fed and bathed.

"Your mother didn't want to leave."

The squeak of a rat and the sound of it scurrying into the wall sent a shiver through him, but it also gave him an idea.

"Run upstairs and get the bottle of the juice Ella gave Dora this morning. The bottle is sitting on the table. Bring it here and do not let anyone drink any."

"Yes, sir," she said and hurried up the stairs.

What if in the last batch Leo made he used the wrong mushrooms? What if he was selling poisonous tonic to the people in Texas?

A few minutes later, Grace came carrying the miracle cure down. The girl moved through life, not really enjoying or having fun any longer. What did he say? Her mother had been gone less than a month. A month was hardly enough time for her to recover. She just wasn't ready.

He found a glass bowl on the counter and poured some of the concoction into the dish and set it on the floor.

"Do me a favor and find me a lock. We're going to close up the cellar until I'm certain this does not contain poison."

Hopefully the rat would help him prove his suspicions. One that had him thinking his sister died of poison and now Dora was very ill. Could it be the miracle cure?

"Yes, sir," she said and scampered back up the stairs. He gathered the charcoal and milk thistle, both good for poisoning.

CHAPTER TEN

Dora thought she was going to die. Now two days later, she was starting to slowly come back to life, and she owed Jesse so much. The man had been by her side, making her drink lots of water, pushing charcoal and milk thistle down her throat. Cleaning and bathing her when she was too weak to care for herself.

Now as she stared out the window, for the first time in days she felt better. Still not strong enough to ride after Leo, but at least on the mend. As much as she wanted to get back on the trail, she needed more rest.

Jesse walked into the bedroom, a tray in his hands. "Time for some hot tea and soup. Let's hope you can keep this down."

When he gazed at her, a blush spread across her face. The man had seen more of her than she intended, but at the time, there was no one else.

How could she ever repay this man? "Thank you, I appreciate everything."

As he set the tray on a table, he helped her scoot up in the bed to where she could eat. "You were ill. I didn't mind. There's something you need to know."

Leaning over her, he tucked a napkin in her nightgown, an intimate act. A tremor or nerves shot through her. Today was the first time she'd been coherent and realized what was really going on in the world.

Jesse moved the small table over to feed her. A quick glance at his face and she realized whatever he wanted to talk about was serious as a frown drew his brows together. A window was open and she heard the children playing outside, their voices shrill as they ran around the yard in the summer sunshine.

"That morning when you came into the kitchen, Ella gave you a cup of her father's miracle cure."

"Yes, I remember," she said between bites. "I barely drank a sip of it. It tasted horrible."

The bitter, oily texture she spit out, and even after she rinsed her mouth, she could not get the dire taste out.

Putting a spoonful of food between her lips, he stared at her, his dark brown eyes filled with concern. "Thank goodness, you didn't. After you showed some of the same symptoms as my sister, I became suspicious."

He fed her a bite of soup and leaned back. "So I went into the cellar to see what they were using in this miracle drink. Grace told me her mother said they were having a hard time finding enough mushrooms. My fear is that they found some poisonous ones. So, I poured some of his tonic in a bowl and left it on the floor."

Another spoonful of soup slipped between her lips. "Not one, but two, dead rats waited for me the next morning."

Stunned, she stared at him. Her husband's miracle cure almost did her in. Wouldn't that have been convenient? Rage caused her to grit her teeth, her hand clenched and she wanted to hit something, anything.

Leo was selling a tonic across the state that almost killed her. "He's going to kill someone."

"He already has. My sister and almost you. Thank goodness I knew enough to give you milk thistle and charcoal."

"I barely had any of the vile stuff, remember? I threw it out," she said in astonishment. How many people would die because of believing this miracle tonic would cure whatever ailed them.

Her hands were so weak, but she pulled herself up higher in the bed. "Tomorrow morning, I'm leaving. Someone needs to stop him."

"Agreed. Since you're so ill, why don't you stay here with the children and I'll go after him?"

Was he out of his mind?

While she would be forever grateful to Jesse taking care of her, she could not remain here with these kids. By the time he got back, she would be thoroughly attached and have to suffer losing them. No way was that going to happen.

With a jerk, she glared at him. "No way in hell. I'm sorry, but for the last two months, I've been training to find him and he's not getting away from me now. You've been nothing but kind to me. Besides, I don't like children. This is something I must do. Find Leo and put an end to our marriage."

She watched as he dipped the spoon and filled it with soup. "Nothing is going to keep me from going after my supposed brother-in-law, including my nieces and nephew. Never doubt, I love them. But their mother deserved so much more than to die because of her worthless husband."

Dora understood his need to apprehend Leo, but she refused to sacrifice to let him have his way. Wasn't going to happen. Her own demons made her want to capture her once-dead husband.

"Agreed," Dora said between the bites of soup he partially shoveled into her mouth.

She could see the wheels churning in his mind and whatever he came up with, there would be some twist that would give him an edge. But it wouldn't matter.

For a moment, he stopped and stared. "Tell you what, I have

an idea. If you're up to it in the morning, we'll have a shooting contest. Whoever hits the most targets, the fastest, that's the person who is going after Leo."

A grin spread across her face. The man had no clue what he was getting into. Unless he was a gunslinger, which she didn't believe, this was a challenge she would easily win.

"You're on. Now stop feeding me soup. I'm feeling stronger, and by tomorrow, I intend to be better and then I'll be heading out without you and the children."

The last thing she needed were three kids straggling along with her. Though she wanted babies so very much, this was not the time or the place.

Placing the spoon back in the bowl, he stood and lifted the tray. "Don't count on it. Not many women can beat a sharpshooter."

"And I'm a fast drawing gunslinger," she said nonchalantly.

CHAPTER ELEVEN

The next morning, Jesse set up tin cans and bottles on the back fence. If he won today, she would stay here and care for the children. From the time he was twelve, he had been shooting a gun and had no doubts he would win. When did she start firing her Colt?

And he couldn't wait to be on his brother-in-law's trail. The man would soon be swinging from a noose.

The kids needed someone to watch over them and he promised his sister to look after her babies and he would. But he also felt the need to settle the score of her death. With so much life left in Ida, it wasn't fair she died from his poisonous concoction.

Turning, he looked up and saw Dora was dressed, sipping coffee, watching him. "Are you ready?"

A grin spread across his face. The poor woman didn't realize what she was getting herself into. His bags were packed and he would be leaving shortly.

Placing the coffee cup on the railing, she walked toward him. A holster rode low on her hips, swaying gently. The woman's blonde hair and sapphire eyes heated his blood and her split riding skirt drew his attention to her center and made his breath catch in his throat.

Though her skin appeared rosy, he was certain she was still recovering from the poison. It was a wonder she hadn't died.

"Do you need to warm up?" she asked.

What did she mean warm up? Jesse would beat her in the first round and be merrily on his way.

The children came out of the house and he called to Grace. "Kids, don't step off the porch. Make certain the baby is being held."

"Yes, sir," Grace replied as she stared at the adults like they had lost their mind.

"I'm ready whenever you are," he said, pulling out his pistol and filling the chamber with bullets.

"Are we timing this?" she asked.

Why would they need to time their shoot off? No need to worry about the legalities, he would win hands down.

"Oh, I don't think we need to," he said, smiling. Did she really believe she could beat him? "Ladies first."

With lightning speed, she pulled out her gun and all five targets were hit in less than five seconds. Stunned, he stared at her as she put her Colt back in her holster. "Your turn."

Cursing under his breath, he wondered how he could compete against her quickness. Sighing, he yanked his pistol out of the holster and the first four bullets landed pretty quick, but the last one refused to go down. That last tin can the bullet whizzed right on by.

A woman had just beat him. Not just any woman, Dora. Now he had good reason never to find himself on her bad side. Poor Leo didn't realize it, but a storm was coming for him.

"Oops," she said, smiling. "Missed one."

With a shake of his head, he stared at her in disbelief while the children clapped and yelled enthusiastically. There was no doubt she beat him fair and square.

Without gloating, she said, "I'm all packed. What you said the other morning while I tried to listen was you thought he would hit Dallas and then head south. To start off, I think that's the trail I'm going to take for now."

"We're going with you," he said. "You've been sick. I can't let you go alone."

"No, you're not. I'll travel faster without you and your brats. Every day I'll get stronger."

The thought of her on the road by herself, searching for Leo without him, left him aching with frustration. No way would he go off and leave the children at the farm by themselves and he didn't have the kids packed.

If he could get to Dallas, he knew his great-aunt Matilda would keep the kids for him, and she would treat Ida's babies like her own. Right now, he didn't want to say anything. Dora needed to believe she was going on her own.

"You're right. We'd slow you down," he said as they walked to the porch where the children stood waiting.

"Wow, you hit all the bottles," Ella said, staring up at her in wonder.

"Thank you. Grace, Ella, and Ben, I'm leaving. Take care of your uncle Jesse. Hopefully, I'll see you again soon," she said, kissing the baby's cheek. Leaning down, she hugged Ella. "Be a good girl."

When she stood, she glanced at Grace, but for some reason the two of them seemed to be at odds. Jesse didn't know why but hoped they would eventually work out their differences. Probably it was simply a girl thing.

"Goodbye, Grace," she said. "Your mother would want you to watch over the kids. But be a little girl and remember you're a beautiful young girl."

"Thank you," Grace said, her voice not at all warm.

"Wait back here," he told the children, suddenly certain of what he wanted.

Dora's horse was saddled and waiting in front of the house. "Boy, you were confident you were going to beat me."

With a smile, she turned toward him. "Just graduated from bounty hunting school. I've had lots of time to practice."

For days now, he wanted to kiss her. From the first night she arrived, during her illness, and now since she won and was leaving, he would take his reward.

Taking her in his arms, he glanced down at her. "You know how bad I want to catch my brother-in-law."

"He's not your brother-in-law. But yes, I realize you want to make him pay, like I do. As his legal wife, you understand, I want to make certain he never harms another woman like he did your sister and me."

That logic was impossible to argue against, and yet, he knew this would not be goodbye. For now, she needed to believe he was letting her win, letting her go after Leo alone.

"All right," he said. "Understood, but you better catch the SOB."

A smile spread across her face and her blue eyes twinkled. "Have no doubts. Leo Tennyson is either swinging from a rope or going to jail. One of the two."

His face leaned down to hers and his lips covered her mouth. Dora tasted of fresh mint and smelled of lavender and the feel of her body next to his had him groaning. The touch of her lips was like a branding iron, leaving him craving and wanting more.

Not that there had been many women, but enough for him to accept this kiss was more than a little special. This kiss heated his blood, swelling his veins and imagining all kinds of things that would find them in trouble. After all, he had seen her naked.

Finally, she pushed back and smiled up at him. "Don't forget, I'm a married woman."

He grinned. "Not for long. Be careful and don't tire yourself. Stop early tonight."

There was more than one reason he wanted her to quit along the trail earlier than she planned. Because this cowboy would load up the wagon with the kids and they would be pulling out not long after Dora.

"I will," she said as she stepped up into her saddle. "I'll send you a telegram when he's behind bars or pushing up daisies."

"You do that," he said, knowing he would be right behind her and she couldn't stop him. Though he was surprised at her reaction to the children. Not many women didn't like kids. Her words said one thing, but her actions were completely different.

Standing in the drive, he watched as she rode her mare down the lane. As she went through the gate, he turned and ran toward the house.

"Everyone, start packing, we're leaving," he said.

CHAPTER TWELVE

Later that evening, Dora sat around her campfire, huddled in her blankets, thinking about their kiss. That kiss reawakened feelings she thought she would never feel again. That kiss reawakened hunger for something she had forgotten about. That kiss left her wondering why he'd given up so easily.

Sure, she won, but the man was obviously stubborn. Even though he agreed the winner would be the one to go after Leo, giving her the right to end Leo's cheating ways. Why then did some niggling little suspicion make her think he was up to something?

A wagon came rolling down the road and she reached for her gun. The sun had already sunk below the horizon. Her fire popped and crackled sending sparks into the sky. The time was long past for decent folks to be out. Suddenly a fussy child began to cry echoing through the trees, and she knew. The child's wailing she recognized as Ben's.

Jesse and his family followed her. Rising, she wrapped the blanket around her and met him as he pulled into her camp.

"I've a good mind to shoot you," she said.

How could he believe taking three children on a hunt was a good idea? They would slow her down, though she knew her body was not fully recovered. This afternoon she'd begun to tire and realized she needed to rest.

"Not in front of the children," he grinned. "Besides, think of the mess."

Her heart leaped at the sight of Jesse and that couldn't happen. All day long, she thought about this morning's kiss and now here he was in the flesh.

"Why did you follow me?"

Jumping down from the wagon, he reached inside the back and helped Grace who held a fussy Ben and then Ella. Before he grasped in the back for the blankets and satchel, he placed the boy in Dora's arms. "You know why. How could I stay home and let you have all the fun?"

With his arms laden with food supplies, she followed him with her load toward the fire. "But the children, they shouldn't go with us."

There was too much danger. Too many risks for them to be riding alongside.

"Agreed," he said, and he looked at Grace. "We're going to visit great-aunt Matilda in Dallas and she'll be happy to keep the kids until we're done."

Grace angrily rebelled. "I don't want to stay with some aunt. I don't know her."

"Maybe it's time you met her. She's family," Jesse sighed and looked at Grace. "On this trip, you can't go with me."

"Where are you going? We could go too," Grace said, and Dora set down the baby and began to set up pallets for the children to sleep on. How would Jesse get out of this one? Gazing at him, she couldn't help but stare at his full lips, the slant of his nose and high cheekbones.

That kiss today left her feeling a little on the curious side. Left her thinking thoughts she had long forgotten. What about anything else with this man? A sigh escaped her. She was a married woman. Though she no longer felt joined as man and wife, the vows she said still applied.

No matter what, she couldn't think of Jesse and her entwined together in the sheets. She just couldn't. Not until this situation with Leo was settled. Though their vows meant nothing to him, she would not disavow the promise she made to God.

Oh, if only she had never married her husband, life would be so much simpler.

"The two of you are going after my father, aren't you," Grace said.

"Papa?" Ella said, looking at Jesse. "You're going to find Papa?"

"Papa, papa, papa," the baby cooed and danced about excited to be out of the wagon. His diaper hung almost to his knees and needed changing. While the children confronted Jesse, she located the bag that held the diapers.

Why was she helping? For everyone, it would be better if he believed she hated kids. No matter what, she couldn't let down her guard and grow attached. These beautiful children weren't hers.

"Come here, Ben," she said, smiling and the baby ran to her and she wrapped her arms around him. "Such a sweet boy."

"Papa," he said, kicking his legs while she changed him.

When she set Ben on his feet, Grace glanced over and saw Dora taking care of her brother. The young girl stomped over to Ben and took him by the hand, leading him away from her. A pain gripped her chest and she didn't understand why. The baby was not hers and his sister only protected him from a woman she didn't like. With a sigh, Dora stood.

"Is anyone hungry," she asked. Obviously, Grace was determined to remain in control. Tonight, she felt too tired to fight her.

"No," Grace said, staring at her uncle. "Answer me, are you going after Leo?"

"Yes," he said.

"Why? To give us back to him? Momma told you not to let papa take us."

Dora didn't envy Jesse trying to explain this one. The children didn't need to realize their father was a crook and they were going to turn him into the sheriff.

If he had a bounty on his head, she'd be collecting the cash and he would be needing an undertaker. And though they both had dibs on who got to kill him right now, it was her choice.

After all, she won the challenge, and yet he followed her, and she planned on killing her dead husband.

"Grace, Leo made that poisonous miracle drink. If he sells that cure-all to people, they're going to die just like your mother. Do you want other children to lose their parent because of that foul drink?"

The little girl began to cry and her sobs broke Dora's heart. This child had been strong and taken on more than most adults could handle. To see the tears flowing down her cheeks, made Dora's chest ache for the pain Grace endured. The suffering of grief and loss no eight-year-old should have to know.

Jesse pulled the child into his arms. "Grace, I'm never leaving you permanently. I'll always come back for you, unless something happens to me."

"No, you can't get hurt, because I don't know what we'd do."

"Aunt Matilda would take you," he said, holding her and speaking softly, trying to calm the young girl.

Grace clung to Jesse. "Find Papa but promise me we'll all go home together. I don't want to live in Dallas with Aunt Matilda. I don't want to travel with papa. All I want is to go home with you."

According to law, the land belonged to Dora. Yet, these three children didn't deserve what life had given them. How could she kick them off the property and send them packing after everything they'd gone through? Now, their uncle and their father's first wife planned on killing Leo.

Even Grace seemed to understand her papa was not the best parent for the three of them.

"Grace, I give you my word, we'll come back."

Dora gazed at Jesse and licked her lips. How many single men would take on the responsibility of three children, one not quite two years old, and yet Jesse stepped in and gladly accepted the care of his sister's family. Would Leo have done the same?

A little snort came from her, oh no. Leo would have packed his bags and ran so fast the other direction, never to be seen again.

These should have been her children, not Leo's. He should be the barren one. Not her.

CHAPTER THIRTEEN

Two days later, they reached the town of Denton and decided it would be best for everyone if they stayed overnight in a hotel room. They were all tired, needed a bath, and Ben was growing cranky at being cooped up all day in the wagon.

And Dora could still feel the effects of the poison. Her body had not completely recovered. The only hotel in the small town had one vacancy, which meant they would have to share a room. Thank goodness the room had two double beds. One for Dora and Grace and one for Jesse, Ben, and Ella.

Only problem was getting all their stuff inside and letting each child have time in the tub. A dressing screen was in the bedroom, and at the desk, they ordered hot water to be delivered to the room.

Once again, Dora helped Jesse get the kids situated. Part of her loved helping with the children, but the protective part knew this would only bring heartache. As soon as they were in bed, she would be jumping into some fresh, clean water.

After leaving their horses and wagon at the livery, they carried all their gear into the hotel. Just as they were about to start baths, a loud ruckus came from outside—a noisy, shouting mob of men carrying torches and firing their guns.

The kids ran to the window while Dora sat out pajamas and a fresh diaper, and Jesse poured the water into the tub.

Standing in front of the glass, Ben began jumping up and down, squealing, "Papa."

Shock ricocheted through Dora seizing her chest as she stared at the three of them and watched as they all became excited.

Jesse gazed at Dora and the two of them heard the girls, shock on their faces. "It's him. Papa. Our Papa."

Panic had her racing to her gun belt she had taken off when they arrived and strapping it around her waist.

"Where are you going?"

"Where do you think? I'm going to..." she glanced at the three little faces staring at her and she couldn't say the words in front of them. No matter what, Leo was their father.

"I'll be back," she said.

"You're not going without me," he said, racing after her. Suddenly he stopped and sent Grace a stern look. "Lock the door behind me and don't go anywhere."

The two of them rushed out the door, into the street. A crowd gathered at the other end of the main road, shouting, guns firing in the air.

In disbelief, she witnessed Leo, the man she believed was dead, slithering down the road. Dora's heart seized with hatred.

Automatically, her hand rested on her pistol as she started toward him. Rage roiled inside her, her chest aching as she thought of the years she believed he was deceased, the missing money, and now those children watching from the hotel room, who all thought of him as their father.

Leo's babies didn't deserve to be rejected this way. Dora didn't deserve to be treated with so little regard. Ida hadn't deserved to be deceived either.

Out of the corner of her eye, she witnessed Ella come running. "Papa, papa."

Leo jerked to a stop and saw Dora and Jesse walking steadily in his direction. His eyes widened with fright and she laid her hand on her gun, her fingers itching to show him exactly what she thought of his lying, cheating ass. Ella stopped in front of him, crying, and he didn't acknowledge her.

"Papa," she cried, tears running down her face. Large, innocent green eyes gazed at him, pleading with him. "Momma died. We need you."

"Go on," he said, pushing the child out of his path. "I can't talk to you right now. Get out of here."

With a shove, he spun his daughter around and pushed her back. The angry mob started down the street where Ella stood in their path. It took every ounce of control to keep from killing him, but tonight was not the time. Not in front of Ella. In fact, she pulled away from Jesse, who put his hand on her arm and ran toward the little girl.

Why had God given him such wonderful children and her nothing but heartache? But she could rescue and comfort Ella. The sobbing child looked petrified standing in the street with a mob of men carrying torches coming at her.

Anger consumed Dora as she ran to Ella and lifted her, carrying her to safety. Dora placed Ella on the wooden sidewalk out of harm's way.

"Why did you leave?" she asked, holding her tightly, trying to comfort her.

The little girl sobbed. "I wanted Papa. I'm so afraid Uncle Jesse won't come back."

Secure in her arms, she rocked the little girl as tears welled up in her eyes. Sometimes life was so unfair. "Your Uncle Jesse loves you. He would never not come back for you. Right now, your papa can't speak to you. Soon, you'll talk to him."

But would she? How could they kill Leo when there were

three children here who loved and wanted their father, even if he was a bad man? Would it be fair to shoot him before his kids had a chance to spend time with him? After all, they lost their mother. They didn't deserve to lose their father as well.

Dora set Ella on the ground and gripped her hand. Together the two of them made their way inside the hotel while Jesse continued to search for Leo.

Why had she ever thought this would be easy? Killing a man, even a dirty-to-the-core one, was not as simple as she believed. Even someone as evil as Leo.

CHAPTER FOURTEEN

With heavy steps, Jesse finally gave up and went back to the hotel room. Seemed Leo's miracle medicine treatment had killed someone in town and a mob searched the streets looking for him. Somehow the man managed to slip through the crowd and probably out of town.

In some ways, a mob killing would have been easier, but the children didn't need to see their father hanged. In fact, seeing Ella's tormented face haunted him. The child wanted her father. Needed him and didn't realize the man she loved was evil. Only that he was her beloved father.

Jesse had grown up with a loving mother and father until they died in an accident. A runaway horse flipped their buggy, killing them both. Even today, he missed their love and wisdom and just hearing their voices.

So how could he in good conscience kill their father? When they learned the truth, how would they feel about what he had done to end his life?

With a sigh, he shook his head and opened the door to the hotel room, expecting to find chaos. Instead the children were all in bed asleep. Behind the bathing screen, he listened to Dora splashing around taking a bath.

The sound sent his heart racing as his mind conjured the image of her naked in the tub. Quickly, he closed down the thoughts. Not a place he should be going with three children in the room.

Jesse cleared his throat to let her know he was back as he searched through his saddle bags for a clean set of clothes.

A few minutes later, she came out from behind the screen, a wrapper around her nightgown as he kept his eyes trained on her face. Unable to look below her neck. Oh yes, he remembered her naked body, very well.

"Did you find him?" she asked.

He shook his head, his disappointment evident in the sag of his shoulders as he thought of the frustration.

"Someone in town, the preacher's wife, died from the juice. That's why the mob was after him. They wanted to hang him," he said. "Somehow, he must have gotten away as I never found him."

"Oh," she said disappointed.

In surprise, he glanced around at the sleeping children. "How did you manage this?"

"Everyone was exhausted. Once they had their baths, we read a story to relax after seeing their papa and they didn't make it to the end."

The woman was a genius. If he had been here, they would still be up and exerting that last bit of energy. "Thank you," he said. "Oh, how I feared coming back and having to give them baths."

A smile crossed her face before she became serious. "The children can't go any farther than Dallas with us."

He knew exactly what she wasn't saying out loud. Tonight's experience had been eye opening. And yet he didn't know what to do. "Agreed."

Shaking her head, she mashed her lips together and said, "I'm going to regret saying this, but they need a chance to see their papa."

Stunned, he stared at her. Was she crazy? Yet, the offer was a kind one. But why would she of all people, the woman who wanted to shoot him, agree to such a request? Staring, he stood thinking of how they would pull that off without her killing the man right in front of the children.

As he gazed at the kids lying in the beds, he couldn't talk about this in the same room with them. Even if they were asleep, he feared someone would be listening and he refused to discuss their father's death now.

"Agreed. But we have to wait to talk about this," he said.

A sense of calm came over him as she nodded her response. Why were things easy with Dora?

"My resolve is unchanged," she said.

Of course, her resolve was unchanged. Probably stronger after seeing him tonight. The man had stolen not only money from her, but years. His lying scheme hurt not only Dora, but his sister and these precious children.

"Understood," he said. "Before the water gets any cooler, I think I'll take a bath."

A smile crossed her face. "I left you a bucket of clean hot water. Hopefully, it's still warm enough for you to enjoy."

One more quick glance at the children, all peacefully sleeping, his heart swelled with love. They were his nieces and nephew and he would do everything he could to protect them and love them, and there was no way he could kill their father. Regardless, he was a huge bastard who deserved to die.

One thing tonight had shown him these kids loved their father and would never forgive him if they ever learned he was the one who killed the ass.

Grabbing his clothes, he headed behind the screen, ready to

scrub the trail dust off and ease his tight muscles. Maybe the bath would help him decide how to capture Leo and keep Dora from killing the man. Or if people continued to die from the miracle cure, he might not have to worry about Dora being the one that ended Leo's life.

CHAPTER FIFTEEN

In the middle of the night, Dora woke to the sound of crying. Sitting up, she realized it was Ella and threw back the covers and went to check on the child. The little girl sobbed in her sleep and Dora sank down on the bed and lifted her into her arms.

"Momma," she said. "I want Momma."

Dora's heart broke at the child's cries. "Shhhh, honey, it's all right. Wake up, sweetie."

Rocking her gently, she wasn't certain if she was crying out or awoke from a nightmare.

"I want Momma," she said again, tears cascading down her face.

Not knowing how to ease her sadness, she simply held her and rocked the little girl while her own tears slid down her cheeks.

She didn't understand why God had taken their mother and left their worthless father. Yet, she couldn't let herself become too attached to Jesse's family. If life was fair, they should belong to her and Leo, not him and Ida.

Regardless, the children weren't at fault because her husband's lying created so many problems. These kids were innocents.

Finally the little girl's sobs quieted, but Dora continued to comfort her. In a soft voice, she asked, "Will I ever see Momma again?"

The question ripped at Dora's soul and she wanted to scream *why this mother? Why this child?*

"Your mom is in heaven. If she could, she would have stayed here with you. When she realized she had to leave you behind, her heart must have been broken. And yes, someday when you die, she will be there to greet you and tell you hello."

While Dora didn't know this with certainty, this child needed answers. "In fact, I bet your mother is looking over you right now and wishing she could hug you and tell you good night."

The little girl nodded. "Momma told us she would always be watching over us. But I would really like to look at her again. I don't want to forget her."

The child's words left Dora's chest aching with pain again. In the darkness, Dora felt tears rolling down her cheeks. "Then don't. Every night or even during the day when you get scared, picture your mother's face. The way she smiled at you when she told you she loved you."

A deep sigh escaped her. "Thank you," she said. "Anytime I have a bad dream, I'm going to think of Momma."

"That's right. She'll chase the bad away. Can you go back to sleep now?"

"Uh-huh," the child said.

"Good." She laid the girl on the bed, covered her, and kissed her on the forehead. "Night, Ella."

The little girl didn't answer, and she became aware she was asleep.

As Dora made her way across the room to her bed, where she lay for hours, sadness filled her as she thought about Jesse's family, understanding she was becoming too involved. Ella clung to her needing a mother figure and the baby too. Both children searching for the loving parent they lost.

Grace understood the realities of death and dying. Dora was just a woman passing through their lives and she refused to even be friends. Grace held a firm grip on her responsibilities and yet she was a child herself.

Waiting for the dawn, listening to the steady breathing of the children and Jesse, she wished they were her family. Oh, how she wanted Jesse and her to share wedding vows and these three kids be a result of their union. But that was a dream and not reality.

Dora still belonged to another man. A woman who believed in the vows of *until death do you part*, she would not consider breaking that bond. Only Leo cheated and tried to take a short cut. Now these children were a product of the lies and schemes of his cheating.

CHAPTER SIXTEEN

As they ate breakfast in a restaurant the next morning, Jesse glanced at Ella. Yesterday had upset the poor kid and last night she suffered nightmares. The woman had comforted the little girl. In fact, at the oddest moments, she would soothe a child. Just like running out into the street and grabbing Ella.

This made no sense.

"For a woman who hates kids, you were up last night comforting Ella," he said.

"Oh, so you lay there awake and let me get up and comfort her," she retorted. "The only reason I got up was to stop the kid from crying."

Dora was lying. Last night, he heard her sniffling as she comforted the child.

"That's why you told her to always think of her momma when she got scared?"

The woman's eyes narrowed. "She's your responsibility, not mine."

"True," he said. "You did a really great job of comforting her."

The scathing look he received should have warned him to

back off, but something between what she said and the way she acted didn't make sense. The two were at odds.

The woman took a bite of her eggs and made a humph noise. "The poor kid was frightened. Seeing her daddy last night really shook her up. This is the kind of stuff you should be prepared to deal with as their caretaker."

As she finished her breakfast, she laid down her napkin and glared at him. "The next time she starts crying in the night, I'll expect you to comfort her. And if we're sharing a bedroom, which, please Lord, not again, I will wake you and say get up and make her shut up."

Part of him wanted to laugh at how upset she was getting. The children always seemed to agitate her, and he didn't understand why. Was it because these kids, except for Grace, belonged to his sister or because of some other reason?

"Why didn't you and Leo have kids?"

For a moment, he feared she would throw her coffee at him as her eyes narrowed and blazed with a heated stare that should have ignited his hair on fire.

"That is none of your business. Like I've said before, I didn't want kids. Still don't."

Something wasn't right and he had yet to figure out what, but she was lying. Eventually he planned on learning everything he could about this woman who intrigued him. The wife of his hated archenemy.

"Where are your kids?" she asked him. "Why aren't you married?"

A simple story. One of duty to his sister. One he would never give up on. One where their father would never take these children from him. They were his now, though he would still like a couple more.

"Raised Ida, built up my business and now that I'm ready to start dating women, boom, my own instant family. Someday I want a son to carry on the family name and a daughter who looks like her mother, whoever that should be."

"So you want even more children," she said.

"Yes, I do. If I have my way, I would like a whole passel of kids on the farm."

For as long as he could remember, he'd dreamed of having a big family.

"Then you better start looking for a wife," she said. "Time's running out."

A laugh escaped him. "Hardly. Who needs to search? When you're as good looking as I am, the women come running. Then you choose the one you want. Unfortunately, I haven't found one I'd say I do with yet."

"Ohhhh," she said, making a mournful sound. "No one makes the man happy. So, so, sad. Better luck next time."

A grin spread across his face and he leaned in. "I'm hoping I'm gazing at someone I want to try out."

Like a porcupine, she bristled and he knew he said the wrong thing. "I don't do try outs."

With a quick glance at the table where the children sat eating, he noticed Grace staring at the two of them. Her forehead scrunched, lips in a frown, her sapphire eyes narrowed.

Of all the children, she had kept her thoughts of her mother's death a secret. Not complaining, not crying--but rather moving through the motions of everyday living, taking care of her siblings. She wiped the baby's face and he squealed with discontent. Sometime soon, Grace needed to become a child again.

While her childhood slipped away, she had become their nursemaid.

He longed for and wanted a wife. Someone to help him raise these children and give him more babies. With a quick glance at Dora, he smiled. The woman would be perfect, if she liked children and would stop acting like a man.

She claimed not to like kids and that seemed odd. Her words didn't fit her personality. But why would she lie?

"Time to get started," she said, rising from the table. "The day is getting away from us and we need to reach Dallas."

She was right. They were wasting valuable daylight and the con man couldn't be that far ahead of them. Once they dropped the kids off at his aunts in the next day or two, the sooner this trip would be over.

Then what? Would Dora kick them off the farm? And if she did, where would they go? His small house could not hold three cats, let alone three children.

CHAPTER SEVENTEEN

Later that night, they finally pulled the wagon over to camp not far from Dallas. By day after tomorrow, they should reach the town and Jesse's Aunt Matilda.

Though she would miss them, Dora would be relieved when the children were no longer there. The baby would come over and smile at her and say Momma, and every time a piece of her heart would splinter off.

While she tried to keep a wall around her fragile emotions, it was getting harder and harder to appear the mean person who didn't like children. When all she really wanted was to grab and love them.

They were Leo and Ida's babies. Not hers and Leo's. She had to keep saying that to herself.

Grace had tagged her as the enemy and the girl did everything she could to keep her brother and sister away from her. Probably, it was for the best and though Dora had done nothing to the child and even tried to help her, she could no longer accept her snotty attitude.

While Jesse went in search of wood and some fresh game, Grace sent her glares across the fire. Finally, she'd had enough.

"I'm not the enemy," she said to the young girl.

"Don't know if you are or not," Grace said, preparing the pallets for the night. "You're not our mother."

That was the problem. Grace was jealous of how Ella and Ben reacted to Dora. "No, I'm not. I'm someone who will soon ride out of your life. So, don't worry about me trying to take your mother's place, because that's not going to happen."

The girl's eyebrows narrowed, and she considered her words. Dora stepped away to spread her bedroll on the other side of the fire away from the children. To make Grace happy, but also to protect her heart, she needed distance.

Tomorrow she would try to spend more time riding and less time in the wagon. They were Jesse's responsibility and he could drive the team.

The thought of Jesse warmed her. Handsome as sin, and even though he'd kissed her once, she had discouraged any further physical touches. With three kids in their midst, it was beyond impossible, plus, she was not the woman he would want. The man wanted children and her womb was as barren as the desert.

"Ben, step away from the fire," Grace called. "Ella, get your brother."

Poor Ella as the middle child, she was always being yelled at. Dora watched the toddler, but the girl didn't move until he started to fall way too close to the flames for comfort. Jumping up, Dora caught him and led him from the fire to his quilt where she showed him his blocks once again.

The snap of a twig had her jerking toward the darkness, her hand on her pistols.

"Daddy?" Ella said, and Dora whirled around to face Leo's pistol.

He was one stupidly brave man to walk into camp with his gun drawn and his children with them.

"Dora," he said, "as you can see, I've risen from the dead."

Rage like nothing she ever felt coursed through her veins and she had to take a steadying breath. "And you're a lot richer."

Leo laughed as his three kids ran toward him and wrapped their tiny arms around his waist. "Hello, kids."

The children loved him unconditionally and he wasn't worthy of their love, their devotion. At the sight, Dora wondered if they'd had children, would he have stolen her money and found another woman?

"Momma's dead," Ella said, standing back staring at him.

"Yes, you told me last night," he said. "Come here, honey, I couldn't talk to you then. Mean men chased me."

Ella reluctantly stepped into his one-armed embrace, he patted her on the head. "You're still daddy's girl."

The manipulation of his own children made Dora nauseous.

"So what are you doing with my kids and why are you following me? The money is long gone and you're never getting your inheritance back."

All the pent-up anger Dora had held onto for the last few months seemed to explode and spew from her mouth. "Yes, I saw that you bought me a nice farm. Though if your *wife* had still been alive, I'm sure we could share lots of notes on how bad a husband you are."

"That doesn't answer why you're following me."

With his children standing at his side, she couldn't tell him she planned on killing him. She couldn't, not in front of them. "Wanted you to understand, I knew you were alive."

"So now I know. Stop following me."

Some things she would keep to herself and surprise him. "You have nothing to worry about unless there's a bounty on your head. Then you better be looking over your shoulder."

Patting his son on his head, he pushed him away. "What are you talking about?"

The man needed shaking up and she aimed to do just

that. "These guns in my holster are there for a reason. A money-making, catching-criminals reason."

A smirk crossed his face as his feet moved backward toward the edge of the woods. Once again, he was going to sneak out of here, leaving his children all upset.

"When I ran out of money, I had to find something to earn me cash. So I trained and became a bounty hunter. Oh how I wish I could arrest you. Until you've got a price on your head, you're free and clear. Look out if you're wanted. Because I will haul you into jail so fast, your head won't have time to spin."

Throwing back his head, his laughter echoed in the camp. "Now that I would like to see."

Jesse who had been hunting fire wood stepped into the light and dropped the sticks as he stared at his brother-in-law. Watching his gun hand.

"Good to see you," Leo said, nodding at Jesse, the pistol still aimed at Dora. "Your sister must have gotten in touch with you before she died."

At first, Jesse didn't respond. "You can't take the children. On her deathbed, she asked me to care for them and I will."

She was proud of the way Jesse stood up to Leo, refusing to let him have the kids, though she doubted he wanted them. His own children were pawns in his game, but mainly they would just get in his way.

Leo smiled. "Always your sister's knight in shining armor. Why didn't you save her?"

Jesse's fists clenched and she understood the pain those words inflicted on him.

"Poison. Your miracle drink killed her."

Shaking his head, Leo unwrapped Grace's and Lee's hands from around his waist. "I don't believe you. Ida helped me make the batch."

"Well, the miracle cure killed her and almost Dora. From what

I heard, your drink also was the end for the preacher's wife in the last town we were in."

The man ran his free hand over his face. "No, you lie. It's not true."

In shock, Leo stood contemplating, his brows drawn together in a frown of disbelief. Maybe he loved Ida; Dora didn't know, didn't have any insight into their marriage. Though Jesse did tell her she said a lot of the same things about Leo that Dora had.

Ida might have found herself stuck - married to a man she didn't care for, just like Dora.

"Daddy, Momma got real sick after she drank your juice. Dora too," Ella said, gazing at her father like she didn't trust him.

Grace glared at Dora like this was all her fault, but she didn't say anything defending her father or her mother.

"No, nothing in that drink should make you ill. Something else made her sick. Ida has been drinking that juice for years. I don't understand what happened."

"Did you pick the right mushrooms?"

In the firelight, his gun hand sagged and the questions were beginning to form. Could she kick the pistol away from him? Taking Leo down was too much of a risk with the children so near him.

Listening to the two men, Dora didn't say anything, but merely stood, wishing he would either put down his weapon or walk away. Right now, with the children present, she would do nothing to harm him. But once they were in Dallas, Leo's life wouldn't be worth the next bottle of miracle cure.

"Don't sell any more of those bottles," Jesse said, warning him. "People will die."

Placing the baby in front of him, he continued to inch toward the woods where he slinked from. Anger rushed through her veins at the way he used his son as a shield. What a coward.

"Cash is king and I need the money," he said. Taking Grace's arm, he pulled her in as a shield. "Make certain they don't follow me."

As he turned and ran into the darkened woods, Grace stared at her and Jesse like she would knock them down if they went after him.

Finally unable to stop herself, Dora glared at Grace. "Relax, I'm not going anywhere in the darkness. There will come a day when I will get my revenge, just not today."

CHAPTER EIGHTEEN

The kids were down for the night. Surprisingly, Dora did not help get them ready for bed. Instead, she walked to the edge of their camp and paced back and forth like a caged animal. Tension radiated from her crossed arms. Her stance was rigid, and the way she strode told him to stay away. Occasionally, he thought he heard her weeping.

Damn Leo for showing up and creating more strain. Grace snapped at everyone. Ella cried and the baby wanted to be held. Normally she pitched in, helping him prepare the children for the night. Tonight, Dora retreated to face her own demons and he would be shocked if she remained here in the morning.

He needed to talk to her and find out what besides Leo she was so upset about. After the kids had finally gone to sleep, he noticed she lay in her bedroll, her eyes wide open as she stared at the stars.

"Gorgeous Texas night," he said softly, not wanting to wake the little ones.

She didn't respond but continued to stare.

"Did you see how he used the children? Especially

Grace? Given a chance, he will train them to be just like himself. Always looking for a way to cheat other people."

Silence.

"How did you two ever marry?" he asked. How could two opposites be united? Then again, Leo had a way of charming women, showing his best side, and after he married them, out came his worst behavior. Jesse witnessed his mistreatment with his sister.

With a sigh, she turned over in her bedroll and leaned on her elbow. "My father. Leo connived my father into thinking he was the man I needed and Papa believed him. Now looking back, my father died suddenly. His death, the reason I received my inheritance. I can't help but wonder if Leo had something to do with his sudden illness."

With a sigh, she said, "How does a young, innocent woman tell her father no? Now look at me. I've gone from living a comfortable life, to being a bounty hunter. Not the life I envisioned for myself. All because I married the wrong man."

Examples of marriage were like dessert or disaster, apple pie or a destructive tornado. While his parents' union had been a happy one, his sister had been a young widow who also tied the knot with the smooth-talking shyster. Yet, as a result of both marriages, she had these beautiful babies. But he could easily see the folly of marrying someone not suitable. A life stuck with a husband or wife that mistreated or didn't love you would be such a waste of years.

Standing, he pulled his bedroll closer to hers and threw another log on the fire as he crawled inside his blankets. Still close enough to watch the children, but where hopefully they could be honest with one another without them listening.

Unable to resist and needing to feel her flesh, he reached over and laid his hand on her arm. "When Leo was here tonight, I feared any moment you would pull out your gun and show him the kind of damage you could inflict. After all, he wouldn't be expecting it from you."

"The thought crossed my mind. There are three innocents who don't deserve to witness such violence. Now if we had been alone, he'd be a dead man."

The thought of her either hanging or spending the rest of her life in prison terrified him. Leo wasn't worth ruining her life over, and yet, the man definitely deserved to be punished. How did you balance evil versus revenge?

No matter what, Jesse wanted to kill Leo for poisoning Ida, but there were three people who depended on him. Three people who he would not let become orphans.

"You can't kill him," he said. "The man has done nothing wrong."

Her arm tensed, and for a moment, he thought she would jump up. "Stealing my inheritance isn't something? Marrying another woman while he's married isn't something? Killing his wife with his deadly miracle drink isn't something?"

If she didn't lower her voice, she would have three little ones asking questions. He hissed. "Shhh! Don't wake the children."

"Oh, I'm sorry, my life has been destroyed. Excuse me for getting a little rowdy. And let's not forget the dead preacher's wife."

The woman had a sharp tongue, but he liked her spunk. And she was right, Leo had stolen so much from her, but she needed to stop and think like a lawman, like a juror.

"Think carefully. Were you married when you received your inheritance? At the time, he was your husband and the law is going to say he didn't steal that money. Because of the marriage, the cash belonged to him to spend anyway he wanted."

The sound of cicadas and crickets and all the night creatures echoed about them. In the firelight, he watched her wiping away angry tears.

"Damn you, Jesse," she whispered. "What you're saying isn't fair."

"I agree, but it's the law," he said. "To be honest, I'm anxious for the kids' sake. You're the legal wife, so if something happens to him, the land will go to you, not the children. All I ask is that you consider their welfare."

Though Jesse would never lie to her, he worried about his nieces and nephew. No, he would never try to steal the property from Dora, but he would make certain they had a place to live. They had lost so much, why should they lose their home as well?

"Well, thanks for being honest with me. But he's still in trouble for bigamy. Remember, he married me and then he married your sister."

Before he said a word, he knew she was not going to like what he would say. Still, she needed to stare the facts in the face, even as ugly as they appeared. "Yes, but Ida is dead. Problem solved. The law is looking for more desperate killers. What sheriff is going to spend their time chasing after a man who likes women?"

While he hated being honest with her, he wanted her to understand the legalities of what she was facing. Right now, they had nothing on Leo. Absolutely nothing.

"So basically, you're trying to gently tell me there is nothing I can legally do to Leo? That he won't be wanted by the law for what he's done to me?"

Slowly he moved his hand down her arm to her hand and he picked it up. "In the eyes of the law, you are still married to him. Not much you can do to him."

"What about your sister's death. Ida died because of his poisonous drink."

"And how are we going to prove that?"

Over and over, he thought about Ida's sudden passing and he wanted to see Leo swinging from a noose. The law would not

DEFIANT

take his word she died from Leo's miracle cure. Until someone else, probably more than one person died, then they had something to convict him on.

Right now, the only thing on Leo was the man was a lying, cheating scoundrel. The world was filled with men like him.

With a quick glance at the children who slept soundly, he sighed. "For their sakes, I want to avenge her death. As much as I want to kill him, I can't. He's their father and they love him. Someday they may learn how truly bad he is, but until then, those kids think he's the best dad in the world."

With a dejected sigh, she dropped her head almost to her chest. "I'm just the woman that showed up and destroyed their last hope of happiness."

Unfortunately, what she said was true. Because if he died, she inherited the land. Right now, there was no reason the law wanted Leo, though two people passed from his miracle cure. Jesse's focus needed to remain on the children. So why was he still pursuing Leo?

"Should we call off the hunt?" he asked, thinking maybe the time had come for him to return to the farm where his nieces and nephew would be safe.

In the firelight, her face appeared a mask of confusion and pain and he realized she would never give up on capturing him.

"I'm going to continue on," she said. "He's not going to give up selling that rotgut poison and people are going to die. Sooner or later, the law is going to go after him and I'm going to get him first."

With a sigh, he laid back and considered his options. She was correct. The miracle cure was killing people, but Leo didn't care. He just wanted the money. Eventually, another innocent would die from the poison. Jesse realized that they needed to stop him, but the only way would be to destroy his drink.

"Maybe, we should go after him with the thought of

destroying the miracle cure. If he doesn't have the product, he can't kill anyone else," he said.

"That's not a bad plan. Long as we reach him in time," she said.

"All right, we'll continue on. Day after tomorrow, we should make it to Dallas, and I'll leave the children there. I promised my sister I would make certain they were taken care of and I will honor my promise to her."

More than ever, he was determined those three kids would have a decent normal life without their father. After what he witnessed tonight, he didn't want Leo anywhere near them.

Before they reached Dallas, Grace and he were going to have a discussion on never putting herself in harm's way again. The child needed to understand her father used her and would continue doing so if she allowed him.

"You will," Dora said, lying down in the darkness, pulling back from him. "I'm married to a man who stole from me, married another woman, and led me to believe he was dead. There's nothing the law is going to do to him."

At the sadness in her voice, Jesse leaned over and stared down at her, the reflections from the fire dancing over her face. "Somewhere soon, he's going to make a miscalculation that will send him to jail."

"Yes," she said. "Even then, I may be attached to him for the rest of my life."

Jesse knew what she said was true, but he didn't want her to remain with Leo.

"Oh, I hope not," he said as his mouth came down on hers. His lips told her what he was feeling, what he could not express. As his lips moved over hers, his heart clenched with a tightness never felt before, and yet, his mind reminded him he was kissing a married woman. That was wrong. No matter that her husband had cheated on her, she remained attached by vows they said in church.

With a reluctance he didn't want to admit, he pulled away from her.

A moment later, she rose and glared at him. "Don't kiss me again, Jesse. No matter what, even if I don't want to accept it, I'm married. My vows are sacred to me. We can't be together."

"Agreed," he said, disappointment curling like a rattler inside him, gripping his stomach. The words she said were true. He didn't want to hear them, and he most certainly didn't want to obey them. Yet, she was right.

With a sigh, she lay down on her pallet and turned her back to him.

Hours passed before he finally fell asleep and dreamed of a blonde woman with sapphire eyes who wore two pistols at her side.

CHAPTER NINETEEN

The next morning, Dora cooked breakfast for everyone while Jesse fed and watered their horses and Ella picked up the bedding, storing the kids' sleeping bags in the wagon. Grace dressed the baby. After seeing her father last night, Grace acted more remote than usual.

"Grace, would you bring me the bread? I thought I'd fix toast this morning," she said as she stood over the fire, frying eggs.

The girl shoved the sack at her, and she glanced at her. "Is there something wrong?"

"Don't think I don't know what you're doing," the young girl said. "You and my uncle are making eyes at each other. He won't leave us for you."

The words and her attitude ticked Dora off. Yes, the child had been through a lot in the last couple of months, but that didn't give her a reason for being rude. And while there were sparks between her and Jesse, they were both well aware she wore a wedding ring and therefore, strictly off limits.

"You're right. Your uncle would never leave you. And I would never ask him to. While he may be making eyes at me, that doesn't mean anything is going to come from this flirtation. I'm married. As much as I dislike my husband, I would never cheat on our vows. Not with Jesse, not with any man, so you're worrying about nothing."

The kid looked shocked. "You're married?"

Dora flipped the eggs, so badly wanting to tell her to whom, but knowing that would only crush the girl even more. What good could come out of Grace realizing her stepfather, the man she adored, was a louse?

"Yes," Dora said almost hissing. "Ever since I came, you fear I'm going to become your mother. I would be honored to have a daughter like you, but it's not going to happen, so you need to stop worrying."

How would the child feel if she learned she was married to her stepfather?

"But you and Uncle Jesse kissed," she said.

Nothing got by this kid. How did she explain that in life you sometimes went the wrong way, but realized you needed to come back to the right path?

"Yes, but that kiss was a mistake. For the last five years I believed I was a widow. Suddenly, I learn my husband is alive and well," she said, hoping she hadn't told Grace too much.

The girl frowned at her. "You came to our house looking for Papa. Why?"

"Because we have business to discuss."

"So why are you still after him? We would all be better off if you weren't here. Why don't you leave?"

That question she asked herself all night. Why didn't she ride off without Jesse and the children this morning? She had no reason to stay and aid him.

Being around these precious kids only reminded her she would never have a family of her own. Not to mention gazing at a tempting man who she wanted to kiss her.

"Maybe I will," she said. "That way, you can help your uncle care for the kids, and I can be on my way. That way you won't be afraid of me becoming your mother any longer. That way, you won't be worried about me marrying your uncle Jesse."

She slid the fried eggs on plates and took them to Ben and Ella who sat on a pallet on the ground watching Grace and Dora, their eyes large.

Then Dora walked over to her sleeping roll and began to pack up her belongings, hoping she would finish before Jesse returned.

Maybe Grace was right. Maybe she just tagged along praying for a miracle. Maybe the time had come for her to strike out on her own. Leaving now, she would no longer be tempted by Jesse and his family. Leaving on her own, if she found Leo, she could kill him.

Somewhere she'd grown soft. After this morning, it was past time to become the bounty hunter she was meant to be. Time to strap on her guns and go in search of the man who needed to be brought to justice, even if the law was unprepared for him.

"Dora," Grace called her voice trembling.

The time for talking was over, Dora had made her decision.

Hauling her gear, she went to her horse and saddled up, grateful Jesse was nowhere around. Because he would talk her into staying and she had overstayed her welcome. This way Grace would have her tight-knit family back. While Jesse took the children to his aunts, she would be on Leo's trail.

Swinging her leg over the saddle, she got comfortable and then kicked the mare's sides. "Let's go, girl. Time to move on."

CHAPTER TWENTY

Jesse walked back into camp and the kids were all staring glumly, picking at their fried eggs. "Where's Dora?"

Grace shrugged, her eyes not meeting his. "Don't know."

A quick glance around and he noticed her sleeping roll, horse, and all her gear were gone.

Gazing at all three of the children, from their expressions, he knew something happened. Ella sat glum faced, staring down at her plate. Even Ben appeared dejected.

"Bye bye," the baby said.

"Grace, you're the oldest. The one I depend on the most. What am I missing here?"

Like she couldn't care less, she didn't respond. The girl's defiant attitude clued him in that whatever happened with Dora, she was being tight lipped.

Finally Ella spoke up. "Grace and Dora got into a fight. Miss Dora decided to leave," Ella said, glancing between Grace and himself.

Just what he didn't need, arguing between his niece and a woman he greatly admired. "Is this true?"

"Yes, sir," she said.

"What were you two in a disagreement about?"

"Nothing," Grace replied.

Staring at each one, he realized Ella knew and she was dying to tell him. Grace sent her sister a withering glare, one that warned of retribution.

"If you don't tell me, I'm going to ask Ella. It would be much better if you told me," he said.

The child gazed down at her feet, her eyes not meeting his.

"She's afraid you're going to marry Dora," Ella blurted out.

"What makes you think that?" Jesse said, wondering why his niece would be upset if he married Dora.

"We saw the two of you kissing," Grace replied, glancing up at him daring him to deny that spectacular kiss.

How could he handle this delicately without making things even worse? Or without losing Dora. The woman had enough spunk in her to fill two women and he wanted her by his side. Now he didn't have Dora and three sets of eyes gazed at him to explain.

"Sometimes a man and a woman kiss. It's a way to see if they like each other."

"Do you like Dora?"

"Well, yes," he said.

"Are you going to marry her?" Ella asked.

"He can't, silly. She's married," Grace said.

Dora told them she was married. But did she tell them to whom? With any luck at all, her husband would soon be dead.

Tears ran down Ella's cheeks, and she wailed.

"Why are you crying?" he asked, thinking maybe this parenting thing was something he wanted no part of.

"I wanted her to be our new momma," Ella said, crying at the top of her lungs.

Standing, he went to her and picked her up in his arms. "She is a nice lady, isn't she?"

"Yes," Ella sobbed as he comforted her.

Somehow there had to be more to this argument than his niece was telling him.

"Why would you object to us getting married? Your brother and sister would have a mother and there might be more children. She would never take your mother's place, but if she made me happy, why would you care?" he said, mystified at Grace's reaction to Dora. "What did you say that sent her running?"

Grace hung her head again and he realized she didn't want to tell him, but Ella's face appeared frustrated and hurt, and she looked him in the eye and said, "She told her to leave. Grace said we would all be better if she weren't here. Why don't you leave?" Ella sighed. "Dora said maybe she should go and she did."

This was the kind of thing Jesse hated. This was the part of parenting he didn't like, but someone had to let Grace know she had overstepped her bounds.

"I'm very disappointed in you, Grace. Last night you let your father use you as a shield so he could escape and this morning, you run off Dora. The next time you cause trouble or disobey, you'll receive a spanking. Are we clear?"

"Yes, sir," she said quietly. "But Papa told me to stand in front of him."

"That was wrong. Leo used you to protect himself from Dora's bullet. No decent father uses their child to hide behind. Do you understand?"

"Yes, sir," she said, tears welling up in her eyes.

"How do you think your mother would have handled this situation?"

No, it wasn't a fair question, but it was a test to see if she realized she had done wrong.

The little girl swallowed before her sister said with delight. "Momma would have spanked her."

Grace glared at her. "Ella," she said in a threatening whisper.

"That's two strikes against you, Grace. One more and you'll be punished."

"Yes, sir," she said.

Jesse still didn't understand the argument, but something sent Dora running.

Had she had enough of the kids? After all, she acted like she didn't want any. Yet, he'd seen her with them, and she would make an excellent mother. First, he had to let the children eat and then he had to try to find Dora and convince her to continue riding with them.

As soon as they reached Dallas, he needed some time to figure out what was going on with Dora and these kids. One moment, she seemed to want to step into the role of their mother and the next she retreated as far as she could.

And she did the same with him. One moment, she was hot and the next cold. How did he cope with a woman like that?

"Eat your breakfast," he said, setting Ella down. "Both of you. We're leaving quickly."

CHAPTER TWENTY-ONE

This morning, she'd ridden off, her emotions all over the place. If she could have her way, she would load up those children and make them hers in every sense of the word. But she had no right.

After riding all day, it was only fifteen more miles to reach the next town. A full day's ride over barren country with few trees and no babbling brooks and the sun beating down on her.

When she started this journey, the prospect of locating Leo seemed so exciting and adventurous and she couldn't wait to catch her husband and do him in.

But now, the thought of killing a man, even a bad one, had been clarified in her mind. After everything, even Leo didn't deserve to be killed and his children made orphans. Part of her felt defeated. She wanted to turn around and go back to Zenith.

But how did she face Ruby and tell her she couldn't even arrest him? She couldn't bring him to justice because the law failed her. As her husband, he controlled their money and therefore the cash was his to purchase what he wanted. In the case of bigamy, his second wife was no longer alive. Now there was just one.

So why did she travel the road alone, out here in the heat, trying to follow him, trying to capture her ruthless husband? What would it gain her?

The western sky was a hue of yellow and orange with a blue tint and she smiled thinking how gorgeous Texas sunsets could be. As she rode into a grove of trees, a shadow moved out of the darkness catching her off guard. She screamed as a rope whirled through the air, wrapping around her chest and arms.

Men reached out and grabbed her horse and her mare whinnied in alarm.

"Stop," she demanded, her hands immobilized, unable to reach for her guns. This was a trap that Ruby had never spoken of, but she had been taught to keep her wits about her and she tried to calm her rapid breathing and pounding heart. Part of her felt angry she'd been so vulnerable.

Yanked from the saddle, she stumbled when her feet hit the ground, but strong arms held her upright. "Are you Dora Tennyson?"

Why would they want her? Part of her didn't want to answer, afraid of their plans.

"Who's asking?" she demanded as she stared at the masked men who had her roped.

"Shut up and answer," the man in front of her said. His handkerchief covered his facial features, and in the gloom, she couldn't tell the color of his eyes.

A bird chirped a happy song in the tree above them and she stared at the pistol pointed at her.

"You're going to kill a woman?" she asked. Why would robbers or rapists want to kill her? Who was searching for her?

"Depends. Are you Dora Tennyson?" the ruffian asked again.

"I can be whoever you want me to be," she said, knowing she was pushing her luck, but why would this group of men be searching for her?

Another man growled. "She looks like who he described."

A scurry of fear trickled up her spine. "Who described? What do you men want? If you're going to rob me, get on with it, but you're going to be disappointed," she said.

A larger man who had been hiding in the woods stepped forward. "Kill her."

Who would want her dead? Like a bullet to the heart, it suddenly dawned on her. The no-good, lousy man she was still married to. Leo. He was the only one who would benefit from her death.

Panic almost overwhelmed Dora.

"Wait a minute. If you're going to kill me, I need to understand why. Don't you think that's fair? I mean, what have I done to you, boys? From the looks of you, I bet you're dying for a home cooked meal. There are some fresh eggs in my saddle, a couple of potatoes and some dried sausage. Are you hungry? I'm a good cook."

Would these men fall for her trick, because there was no way she would cook for them. The moment her hands were loose, they were going for a spare gun she carried in her boot. They wouldn't get to enjoy the meal she described.

The men started to mumble between themselves. She overheard a man say, "We ain't being paid much for this job. Why not enjoy a home cooked meal?"

Assessing the situation, she could only see three men.

"Jed, I'm sick of your cooking. Let's let her fix us some supper. We'll finish the job in the morning and head back to town."

"I don't know," the leader, said.

"I'm with Roy. Let's eat a home cooked meal and take a peek beneath that split skirt of hers." A gross man grinned at her.

She would shoot him first. The man would die with his hard on.

The three men stared at her. Then the leader stepped in front of her and removed the rope. "Just a minute," she said. "I'm doing you a favor, now obviously you've been hired for a job. You should tell me who hired you."

She needed to know if Leo would actually hire someone to kill her. She needed confirmation of his evil deed.

"No, not a good idea," the man who smelled like he took a bath only once a year said.

"Leo Tennyson," a man said, walking to her saddle bags, opening and going through them. "Found the eggs and the skillet."

As they raised the rope over her head, they made a huge mistake not removing her guns. Her hands reached for her pistols, yanking the guns out as she shot the two at close range. The bang ricocheted through the small area with the look of surprise on her victims' faces.

"Never underestimate a woman."

The third man, she whirled on and he stared at her, his eyes wide, his hands stretched high. "No, ma'am. Don't shoot me."

"Drop your guns in the dirt," she screamed. "Now. Don't give me a reason to pull this trigger."

He obeyed and she kicked them out of the way. "Why shouldn't I kill you," she said, walking around him, fear and anger charging through her. "You were going to check under my skirts and then kill me. You were being paid to end my life."

Why did it seem like this man wanted her to show him mercy when he had no plans on giving her any? Had they lived, they would've eaten the meal she'd prepared, raped and killed her. So why should she give him a second chance?

"Ma'am, I have a wife and two kids at home."

"And you think that makes me feel more lenient? That I won't kill you because of your family?" She leaned in close, but not too close. "What about my life? What about my family?"

"You don't have anyone," he said. "Leo told us you were barren."

Fury rolled like a tidal wave through her and she pulled the hammer back on her gun, her eyes filled with tears of rage. How dare Leo tell strangers her situation. The man started crying.

"You, ass, I want to kill you so badly, but you remember that I'm going to let you live. I'm going to haul your sorry butt to the sheriff where you're going to tell him that my husband hired you to kill me. Then if I ever see you again and you aren't obeying the law and being a good man, you'll be a dead one. Do you understand me?"

"Yes, ma'am," he said, shaking.

Now at least, she would have a bounty on Leo. Now she would have a reason to kill him. Now no one could stop her. Seemed like his ploy to kill her had just backfired on him and brought about his own death.

"Put your hands behind your back," she said. "And don't try anything or you will be a dead man."

The man complied and she quickly reached down for the rope inside her boot and wrapped his wrists tightly. When she finished, she found the skillet and began to make a fire. After all this work, she was starving.

The idea crossed her mind that maybe she had apprehended her first bounties. Wouldn't Ruby be proud of how she handled herself today? Obviously, her training paid off.

Tomorrow she would stop in the next town and turn the bodies over to the sheriff and turn in her captured fugitive. Then she thought of Leo. Wouldn't he be surprised when he saw her again.

A noise in the brush had her pulling her gun, just as Jesse walked into the light of her fire. "What the hell, Dora?"

Part of her was happy to see him. But the children...she didn't know if she could continue.

CHAPTER TWENTY-TWO

*J*esse stared at the two bodies on the ground and the poor man sitting with his hands tied behind his back.

"What happened?"

"Leo hired these men to kill me," she said, throwing another log on the fire

As he gazed around at the scene, his heart stopped. What if he had ridden into her camp with the children and found her dead? Didn't Leo ever think about his kids and how seeing Dora killed would have affected their lives? Was the selfish man so intent on getting rid of his first wife, he thought nothing of the family he left behind?

Leaning down, he searched for a pulse on the two men. Dead. Shot in the heart; they died instantly. "How come he's still alive?"

"Roy, here was going through my saddle bags, giving me the opportunity to cook them a good meal before they checked out my lady parts, then they were going to shoot me. They never expected me to draw on them."

The poor fools had no idea what and who they were up

against. The woman could out shoot most men, so they didn't stand a chance.

"What are you going to do with the bodies?" he asked.

How did he explain this to the children and did he want to? While he understood her shooting the men for trying to kill her, he wasn't used to having to deal with gunmen.

Jesse was just a poor carpenter who did a little farming on the side. Chasing after outlaws was not the type of life he expected or wanted, and for a woman, she seemed to be dealing with it exceptionally well.

"Well, since you're here, if you don't mind helping me put them up on the back of their horses. Tomorrow, I'm taking the bodies into town and I'm going to see if there is any bounty on them. If so, I plan to collect my very first reward."

Roy jerked and pulled at the ropes on his wrists. The man obviously had a price on his head, the way he kept trying to slink away into the night.

"Now, Roy, don't make me tie you up even more. Seems you didn't like the idea of being hauled into the sheriff," she smiled. "You got a bounty on your head."

The man didn't answer. "Looks like tomorrow is going to be payday for me."

Why did he find this whole situation kind of unnerving? What prompted her to leave this morning? Was it the fight with Grace, the most stubborn temperamental child he had ever encountered?

Gazing around the camp, he knew he needed answers. "Why did you ride off without us this morning?"

Her giddiness immediately changed and she sighed. "It's for the best, Jesse."

How could she think riding alone without him and the children was better than riding together? How could he go another day without her by his side? Today, along the road, he searched for her and then when he found her, fear spiraled through him. What if she had been killed?

"You're wrong," he said, his frustration escaping. "Ella told me you and Grace got into a disagreement. But I'm still not certain what sent you out on your own. It doesn't make sense. We were working together."

Or at least, he thought they were hunting Leo. Why did he get the feeling she wanted to go out on her own?

"It's your children," she said, her voice raising. "The baby who crawls up in my lap and says momma. Ella who is so sweet and is missing her mother so much and then there's Grace. She wants me gone because she fears I'm going to marry her uncle. Which I explained to her, I'm married. That pacified her, but I can't do this anymore."

There was something he didn't understand. She said she didn't like children and yet when she described his nieces and nephew it sounded like she cared about them.

"I thought you enjoyed being around them," he said.

"No, I can't enjoy being around them," she said, her voice rising, a stricken look on her face.

In amazement, he saw the tears swelling in her eyes as confusion overwhelmed him. What part of this didn't he understand?

The man sitting near the dead bodies suddenly spoke up. "She's barren."

Dora's head jerked up and before he could stop her, she pulled out her gun and shot close to the man's feet, the bullet sending up a shower of dirt and rocks. "Shut up. The next bullet will hit your heart."

Jesse's chest tightened with disappointment, aching in pain.

Now he understood why she didn't have any babies with Leo. Now he understood why she didn't like children. Now it all made sense and anguish consumed him. In the darkest corner of his mind, he hoped eventually she would accept him.

Not now, not until Leo was gone, but he wanted her, and yet, he longed for his own kids. A son who looked like him, a daughter who had her mother's features.

Dora could never give him what he wanted, and she had erected defenses to keep the children from getting too close to her. Only occasionally those walls would come down and one of the kids would get to her.

"Is this true?" he asked.

Tears welled in her blue eyes, glittering with pain. "Yes. I can't have babies."

Sinking down on the ground beside her, he tried to take her in his arms, but she pushed him away.

"Don't," she whispered. "Just go. Tonight, I'll sleep here. You and the children make camp somewhere else."

"Dora," he said, wanting to comfort her.

"Just go," she said. "Tomorrow, I'll be better. Tonight, I can't deal with the fact my husband hired these men to kill me and also your beautiful children. Give me some time."

Rising to his feet, Jesse sighed. This woman was more complex than any woman he ever met, and he admired her spunk, her fortitude, and her strength. And yet tonight, he'd seen a vulnerable side of her that left him reeling.

CHAPTER TWENTY-THREE

Some nights were easier than others. Last night had been gut wrenching with a stranger there to witness her despair. After she fired a gun at him, the man smartly remained quiet the rest of the night. This morning she found him curled in a ball on the ground sleeping, a sense of wrongdoing overcame her.

Maybe she acted a little heartless. If the outlaw had kept his mouth shut, she wouldn't need to explain to Jesse why she couldn't be around his children. Today, she would need Jesse's help in getting the dead bodies and the man to the nearest town.

And Leo. Right now, an arrest warrant didn't matter. The fact he told these men she was barren ate at her like an ulcer. Nothing like letting the whole world know your business. In the predawn, she awoke with a clear head and a determined heart. Her soul burned with anger toward her husband.

When she turned the men in, Roy would corroborate her story that Leo hired them to kill her. Most of the time, the law didn't worry too much about women, so it might not matter. Even if the sheriff didn't care about her life, she would still make certain the jerk didn't live long.

The sound of Jesse riding into camp had her turning to him. This morning, she needed to act like nothing was wrong. That everything was fine. Last night, he'd seen her at her most vulnerable. Today, she would smile and pretend everything was peachy. Inside, her heart ached, on the outside, she would wear the brightest grin.

Now he knew her secret, her shame, her utmost desire.

"Good morning," she called, a smile in her voice.

Confusion radiated from his eyes as he gazed at her, searching her face, and she smiled to reassure him, though she still felt broken.

"Did you sleep well?" she asked.

Concern crossed his face. "Ella had another nightmare."

"Is she all right?"

"She wanted to come with me to see you. I told her no. Maybe later, if you would talk to her."

Pain gripped her chest. The child wanted her, but could she be close to her again?

Ella was quickly becoming her favorite. The little girl's sweet innocence and tenderness wrapped its tentacles around her heart, and no matter what, she could not shake them loose. Yet when they parted, they would never see each other again, and she would be the one left hurting.

"Later, I'll talk to her," she said, her voice almost cracking.

"Are we riding together?" he asked.

What could she say? They needed one another at the moment, and soon, the children would be at his aunt's. After they found Leo, she would walk away from Jesse and his family.

"Yes," she said with a sigh that she tried her best to make happy. "We need to get on the road."

"Let's load up the bodies on horses and we'll lead Roy on his horse. I'll go back to camp and load up the children, then we'll head into town."

Stepping out of his saddle, he stood in front of her, gazing into her eyes and her lungs seized. Something drew her to Jesse. Something about this kind, honest man, and yet, she would be the worst person for him as he wanted his own family. An impossible request for her.

His fingers reached out and brushed a piece of her blonde hair back. "I am a stupid fool."

Stunned, she gazed at him. "Why?"

"After being married to Leo for five years, I should have known why you had no children. When you tried to tell me you didn't like children and I saw how much you cared about them, I should have known. So many clues right in front of me and I didn't realize the problem."

The anguish inside of her exploded, and she closed her eyes. His fingers lifted her chin and she opened her eyes as his lips came down on hers. It was a kiss that spoke of pain and suffering and healing. It was a kiss that promised forever. A promise that would never be delivered.

Yet, she enjoyed the feel of his mouth against hers, the way his heart raced as they touched. The smell of him this close. There was so much she liked about this man and she couldn't become involved with him.

Stepping back, breathing heavily, she shook her head. "We can't. I'm married. Besides, I will never be the woman for you."

He stepped toward her, his hand reached out to touch her and then dropped. "Let's just get through this. Afterward, we can talk about what happens next."

As he walked away, she sighed. No, they would never discuss what happened next because his dreams were just as important as hers. And he wanted something that would only break her heart and leave him disappointed. As soon as they captured Leo or killed him, she would be on her way.

CHAPTER TWENTY-FOUR

Jesse slept very little last night and now today as he drove the wagon into the small settlement, disappointment and exhaustion rode him hard. Yet, Dora sat her horse, her back straight, her head held high and all the puzzle pieces of this woman seemed to be coming together.

No wonder she reacted to his nieces and nephew the way she did. Part of him felt broken. Having his own family had been his dream for so many years.

Traveling with Dora, he began to think that maybe he had found a woman he could love for eternity. Now he was a mass of confusion.

When they pulled up in front of the sheriff's office in Fremont, Texas, he set the brake and turned to Grace. "Stay in this wagon. Don't move. If you get out, there will be serious consequences."

"What's conseces," Ella asked.

"A spanking," he said, glancing at Grace. "You're in charge."

"Yes, sir," she said.

Dora stepped out of her saddle and walked toward the door to the sheriff's office. He quickly followed her inside. They had covered the dead bodies with blankets to keep the children from seeing the men.

"Can I help you?" the small-town sheriff asked.

"I've got two dead men, plus Roy outside that I want to know if there are any bounties on them."

The man looked at her stunned. For the next twenty minutes, they explained what happened and then the sheriff stood and followed them out the door. As they walked outside, Jesse noticed the wagon was empty.

Cursing beneath his breath, he left Dora to deal with the law. He had three stragglers to find and he just prayed their father was not in this one-horse town.

Searching up and down the street, when he walked around the corner, Leo had Ella standing on a box with him.

"This is my daughter and she is going to take a sip of my miracle cure to show you I have my own kids drinking this stuff."

His heart jumped into his throat, his stomach cramping with panic as he ran toward the horse and pony show. Damn Leo for doing this to his own children. Why would he risk their lives if he loved them? Why?

"No, Papa," Ella said, shaking her head. "I don't like the taste. Remember what happened to Momma."

Leo's face turned red and he smacked her bottom and whispered something to her. Terror gripped him and Jesse ran as fast as he could.

"Stop," he screamed. "Stop. Ella, don't drink that stuff. You know what it did to your mother."

The child glanced up at her father and poured the liquid on the ground. "No, Papa. No."

Pushing through the gathering of people Jesse looked at the crowd. "My sister died drinking this miracle cure. Don't buy this poison. Go home."

Leo tried to punch Jesse, but he grabbed his hand, twisting it behind his back. "You're a cold-hearted bastard. Where are Grace and Ben?"

The man ignored him. "Stop."

"Where is Ben?" he asked Ella who was staring at him, her eyes wide, her bottom lip trembling.

Grace came from behind a building holding Ben's hand. "What's wrong? We just came to hear Daddy."

Not wanting his nieces and nephew to witness what he'd like to do to their father, he dropped Leo's arm, who shook the limb and glared at him.

"Young lady, I told you to stay put. Now take the children and get back to the wagon, right now. You will be punished."

Her face went white with fear. "I'm staying with Papa."

"No, you're not."

"Honey, if you want to travel with me, you can. I'm your father. This is just your crazy uncle," he said, packing up his wares.

Oh, Jesse was crazy all right. Crazy enough that he walked over to Leo and whispered, "Dora is at the sheriff's office right this moment, with the three thugs you sent to kill her. Two of them are dead from her gunshots and the third is in there singing like a bird."

Leo's eyes widened.

"She's trying to convince the sheriff to issue a warrant for your arrest because of your hired murderers. If you're a smart man, you will hightail it out of town as fast as possible. Taking three kids with you is only going to slow you down."

The man's eyes grew large and Jesse knew fear gripped Leo as he started throwing his stuff into his wagon.

Leo stepped in front of Grace. "Honey, now might not be the best time for you to go traveling with your papa. But we'll do it real soon."

His words were a lie and sooner or later, the children were

going to figure out their father could not be trusted. Sooner or later, he was going to hurt one of them, if Jesse wasn't careful.

"You've got five minutes before I tell the law."

"Gotta go, sugar," he said as he jumped in his wagon, clicked to the horses, and left his three kids standing in the dust.

It had taken every ounce of strength inside Jesse to keep from killing him, right here and now. But soon, Leo would be in front of him without his children protecting him. Soon nothing would stop him from either capturing or destroying Leo.

"Dada," Ben said, frowning as the wagon drove off.

Jesse turned on the kids, their questioning eyes staring up at him. Being a parent was turning out to be the hardest job he'd ever held. They were innocents in a game he was trying to protect them from.

"Grace, you will receive a spanking for not minding me tonight."

"Uncle Jesse, we saw Papa and came to say hello," she said.

"And he tried to give your sister some of that vile juice he's selling. Next time, you will mind me."

Tears welled up in her eyes, but he refused to let them affect him. The sight of Ella and the glass of dreadful poison frightened him. Hopefully, he scared enough people today to stop them from buying Leo's miracle cure. Hopefully soon, Leo would be crafting cons from prison or swinging from a rope.

CHAPTER TWENTY-FIVE

*D*ora walked out of the sheriff's office, smiling. For the first time in her life, she had earned some cash. The two dead men were wanted, and once Roy confirmed they had been sent to kill her, the sheriff happily paid the bounties.

Counting her money, she couldn't help but want to do a little dance in the street. A thousand dollars would go a long way toward her remaining in Zenith. Tonight, she would splurge, and they would all stay in a hotel and even eat a meal at a restaurant.

Looking up, she watched Jesse, a frown on his face, holding Ben in his arms with Elle's hand in his and a sullen Grace following him marching back to the wagon. Right now, the scowl on his face would frighten even goblins.

"What's wrong?"

"We'll talk later," he said. "What happened with the sheriff?"

Definitely something put a strained expression on not only Jesse's face, but the children's as well.

She held up a stack of bills and his eyes widened. "All of us need a night sleeping on a mattress, not the cold, hard ground. Especially since we should reach Dallas tomorrow. We can get baths and have dinner at a cafe."

"No," Jesse said and she frowned at him. "Let's spend the night, but no trips to a restaurant. That would be a treat, and no one obeyed me today. As punishment, we're not eating out tonight."

Stunned, Dora gazed at the children, the disappointed looks on their faces disheartening. Whatever took place had to be really bad, because the grimace on Jesse's face warned them to behave.

"But Uncle Jesse, I'm hungry," Ella cried.

"Did you stay in the wagon like I said," he asked.

"No," she whimpered.

"You're lucky to get a sandwich. After baths, everyone will go to bed," he declared.

Whatever happened, Dora could see Jesse was plenty upset with his little family. Grace stomped past him and hauled herself into the vehicle, turning away from him, refusing to help him with the little ones. He lifted Ella and then the baby, before he climbed into the driver's seat.

"There's a nice hotel right down the street," Dora said, thinking she needed her own room. The atmosphere crackled with tension and Grace already didn't approve of her. Whatever transpired, the young girl's eyes radiated almost hatred and her mouth puckered into a pout.

Just as darkness fell, they checked into the hotel with two rooms. Jesse and the children stayed in one room and Dora in another. Alone she was happy. A door separated their rooms where the kids could come in any time.

Dora helped Jesse feed and bathe Ben and afterward, she went to her own room where she prepared for bed. Last night, she had very little sleep and needed to catch up on her rest. After her bath, she changed into her nightgown, her robe lying at the foot of the bed.

Soon, she heard a light tap on the door. Getting up, she wrapped her wrapper around her and opened the door.

Jesse stood there in pants, no shirt, his hair wet from his bath.

"We need to talk," he said, walking into her room, pacing the small space in his bare feet.

"All right," she said. "From the scowls on your face this afternoon, I knew you were upset. What happened?"

Dora listened as Jesse told her about how he had found the children with their father. The spanking he gave Grace this evening for disobeying, how Leo had tried to use Ella.

"He's going to keep on until someone else dies."

Rage consumed her like an abandoned house fire, her hands curling into fists.

"By the time I got there, Ella kept saying 'no Papa, no' as he tried to persuade her to show the people his miracle cure was good," Jesse said, pacing the floor. "How dare he give that poison to his own kids, after his wife died?"

The man was a monster, but his children loved him. Why couldn't she have married someone like Jesse, a man determined to protect and raise his sister's babies? Why did she have to marry a man who she believed was crazy?

Seeing how frightened and tense Jesse appeared, she rubbed her hand on his back as he stared out the window.

"You stopped him," she said, wishing she had been where Leo was selling his poisonous miracle cure.

"Yes, I told him, at that moment, you were talking to the sheriff. Telling how you killed two of the men he sent to murder you and that the third one was in the office singing to the lawman. He packed up his miracle cure and rode out of town without the girls," he said, sighing.

"Thank goodness for that."

"At first, he was going to take Grace, but when he learned about you speaking to the sheriff, he changed his mind." Jesse's fist clenched. "Right there in front of his children, I so wanted to hurt him, but knew that would be wrong. And he used those kids to his advantage."

Turning toward her, they stood staring at each other, the tension palpable. In the glow of the light, his arms slipped around her and he pulled her against him. "I'm sorry about last night. All day, I waited for a chance to tell you I'm sorry."

Her heart wrenched with pain. Oh, how she wanted this man, but she could not give him what he longed for in life and he deserved his own family. "It's not your fault."

"No, but I'm sure in the last few weeks I've said or done something to make you feel even worse about your situation," he said, holding her to where she melted into him.

Standing in her robe, his chest bare, his scent overwhelmed her. The beat of his heart slammed against her own, her breathing increased, and her blood heated in the center of her body. Leaning back, he stared in her eyes, her mouth dried up and her words did too.

Oh, how she wished her life was different, that she wasn't a married woman, that she could give him what he longed for, a family of his own.

His lips descended toward her and she put a hand on his chest. It took everything in her to stop him. "No, we can't. I'm married."

"Dora, your marriage is nothing. The vows you said meant nothing to Leo."

Yes, it was true, but she would not break her vows. They were her word, her promise, and regardless that her husband didn't care about them, she did.

"I know, but we said the words in a courthouse in front of God and everyone. And I'm not going to be the one to make a mockery out of them. Yes, he cheated, but until the day he takes his last breath, I refuse to go against my revered wedding vows," she whispered. "You and I both know I can't give you what you truly want. A son of your own."

The pain radiated through her, almost crippling with the hurt, but the words had to be said.

Stepping out of his arms, she turned her back to him, her voice cracking. "Please go."

CHAPTER TWENTY-SIX

$\mathcal{A}$s Dora drove the wagon through the streets of Dallas, Jesse rode in front of them, leading.

Dora knew she needed to say something to Grace. The girl had barely spoken all morning. "Grace, there's something you need to know."

The child turned toward her and gave her a look that clearly said she wasn't interested in anything Dora had to say. "I think you're old enough to understand what's going on in the grown-ups' lives that has brought you to this place."

Since yesterday, Grace had been petulant and mean spirited, refusing to help anyone. Maybe the time had come to give her a life lesson that showed her the truth.

Dora watched as she shifted a little more in her seat, turning to hear her. "Years ago, I was forced to marry a man I really didn't love, but he convinced my father he was the best man for me.

"Because Papa wanted me to, and as women we obey our fathers, I married him. We were together for five years and I never conceived a child. All the time, he blamed me for not getting pregnant and giving him the son he wanted."

She took a deep breath as all the painful memories came back at the way he screamed and yelled at her. Blaming her that he didn't have a son. "One day, my father died suddenly, and I inherited a lot of money. Not long after the funeral, my husband took a trip to Dodge City, Kansas."

Clicking the reins, she urged the horse on and glanced at the girl who stared at her wide eyed. "Several weeks after he left, I received a telegram telling me he was killed in a shootout and they buried him on Boot Hill. Later, I went to the bank to withdraw some cash and learned most of my money was gone."

The young girl gawked at her. "What did you do?"

"The banker said my husband withdrew our money. When I contacted the sheriff of Dodge City, he told me my husband played poker and lost everything."

Dora remembered that terrible day and all the pain came bubbling through her. There had been enough money in the account to last them the rest of their lives and yet somehow Leo squandered it all on cards, except for the land.

"Once again, I was a free woman. Someday, I dreamed, I would remarry and have the family I wanted. In the meantime, he left me just enough cash for me to survive for a while. Five years later, the sheriff of Zenith, where I live, told me he'd seen him in town."

"How can that be? He's dead."

"That's what I thought until I saw him." The words hung in the air, neither of them saying a word until she could see the dawning on the child's face. Only eight, the girl was smart, and she obviously understood the man she adored was not a great man.

"Leo met mother in that town," she said, turning to Dora, she stared at her, tears in her eyes. "Is Leo your husband?"

"Yes," she said quietly. "This is one of the reasons I could never be with your uncle Jesse who is a fine man. But I'm still a married woman."

The girl's head dropped, and she wiped her eyes. "I'm sorry."

"It's all right. You don't have to worry about me taking him away from you. Because I can't."

"Papa married Momma and they had Ella and Ben," she said perplexed.

"Yes, Leo received the son he always wanted with your mother." As much as the words hurt to say out loud, she adored Ben and Ella.

"But..."Grace said, confusion on her face. "So, Momma never was married to Leo?"

"Not legally," Dora said gently.

During this trip, she honestly thought the veil had been lifted from the child's eyes and she was starting to see Leo for the monster he was.

"You can't have children," she said.

"No," Dora replied her chest aching. No longer could she blame her barrenness on Leo. "Once we find Leo, this will all be over, and you and Jesse can take Ella and Ben home."

A pang of guilt radiated through Dora. That land actually belonged to her, and as of now, she had made no decision on what she was going to do about selling the property. The kids would be devastated if they couldn't return home.

Jesse stopped and Dora pulled the wagon in front of a nice home on the east side of Dallas. Far enough from the downtown area, but not out of the city either.

"Wait here," Jesse said as he rushed up to the door and knocked.

"While you're here, watch over your brother and sister and don't let anything bad happen to them. If Leo comes around, don't go near him."

Grace reached over and touched her arm. It was the first time the child touched her, and she gazed at the innocent young girl. "I'm sorry that happened to you. Leo can be very mean sometimes. He used to hit Momma."

This was something Dora was certain Jesse didn't know.

"No man or woman should ever hit anyone," Dora replied.

"She loved him, and he took care of us. Though they often argued late in the night," she said, sounding more like a teenager than a child.

More than anything, Dora wanted Grace to grow up and love a man worthy of her, who would treat her right. "Remember these things, and when your time to marry comes, be certain you're choosing wisely."

An older woman answered the door and gazed out. They sat in the wagon watching as she spoke to Jesse and then hugged him around the neck. He motioned for them to come to the door. Dora stepped down and then reached in the back for a sleeping Ella and Ben.

Gazing at them, she let her eyes drink them in, because as soon as they found Leo...this could be the last time she saw them. It would be in her best interest to put as much distance between them as possible because her heart was becoming attached to them. Jesse, as much as the children.

And it would never be good for her to become involved. That would only lead to her experiencing more pain and disappointment. Something she didn't need any more of.

CHAPTER TWENTY-SEVEN

They visited with his aunt Matilda for over an hour before they made their way to the door. When the children learned they would be staying, they had not been happy. Especially, Ben who let everyone know his displeasure as they walked out.

The poor guy's world had been in total upheaval for so long, and another person leaving him was more than he could take. The boy lay on the floor, kicked and screamed at the top of his lungs, and Jesse's heart shattered walking out the door.

Dora's eyes filled with tears and he feared she would break down crying herself. For a woman who would never be a mother, she had all the natural instincts.

Some days she let down her guard and gave them the attention they needed. Then there were the times he could see her stepping away, putting distance between them so she wouldn't feel the pain when she departed.

All along, in the back of his mind, he'd been thinking *wait, just wait until this is over*. Then he would show her his intentions, because he wanted her more fiercely than a drunk wanted his next drink. The thought of slipping into her arms and letting his mouth caress hers kept him awake at night.

And yet now, the news she was barren shook him to his core.

For he dreamed of having his own family, his own sons and daughters to play with his sister's children. The house would be filled with children and babies, and the woman he loved and he would create a happy home. With Dora, that dream was not a possibility. Could he give up his desires for Dora? Did he want to give them up for this strong woman?

A woman who would stand by her values and honor her vows. Because he wanted to ignore her wedding vows and she told him quickly even if her husband hadn't honored their promise before God, she would.

That took an honorable person to uphold, after being betrayed so badly by Leo. For five years, she thought of herself as a widow only to wake up one day and learn her worst nightmare still lived.

Today, watching her making certain the children had everything they needed and the way she gave them each a hug as she said goodbye, rattled him. It was like she didn't plan on ever seeing them again.

Leo couldn't be that far ahead of them. Sooner or later, this would end and while he knew what he hoped would happen, nothing was certain.

They traveled south, hoping to reach the next small town before dark, but finally stopped along the trail. Tonight, they made camp under the stars, their bedrolls close but not touching.

"Do you think the children are all right," she said in the darkness.

"Aunt Matilda is the grandmother everyone always wishes for, but seldom get. After we left, they were going to make cookies. How many kids don't like cookies? Tomorrow, she's taking them with her to church. She made a list of things they were going to do together. They may not want to go home."

These poor children had experienced so much in the last month, he feared they would be forever traumatized. Especially Ben. The baby kept asking for his momma and the sound of his crying felt like a knife opening a wound every time.

"Grace and I had a talk today," she said. "As we drove, I told her about my husband."

"How did she respond," he asked, wondering if that was such a good idea. "Actually, she recognized the man I spoke about was Leo. She confided in me that Leo hit your sister and they often argued."

Just what Jesse didn't want to know. He always suspected Leo was a hitter, but he treated Ida very well in front of company. Still, how could any man slap or punch a woman? Jesse never understood.

"Leo has a lot to answer for. More than you and I can ever make him atone for. Maybe we shouldn't be chasing after him. I keep wondering if we shouldn't let him ride off and let someone else do all the dirty work. Eventually, someone who is going to kill him."

A moment of silence stretched between them as the cicadas sang a lonely song searching for a mate.

"I've considered that myself. Then I think we've got to stop him from selling all that miracle cure. Even if we have to break the bottles. If he sells that stuff, someone is going to realize his drink killed their loved one."

Dora was right. Their mission had gone from capturing and killing Leo, to putting him out of business. But a tiny voice didn't think a woman spurned as badly as Dora would ever give up on putting an end to a man who had stolen money from her, lied about his death, and created a second family. And he couldn't blame her.

"So, is that what we're doing?" he asked, wanting to hear her say the words, not believing for one minute she had given up on ending his life.

"Yes, I don't want to go to jail for killing him. What about your sister's death? You ready to give up on Leo after he killed her, and accept her death?"

Jesse paused and considered her words. As much as he believed he shouldn't kill Leo, the desire rode him hard.

"No, I plan to avenge her death."

Dora laughed. "I realized you were lying, just like I wasn't telling you the complete truth. No, he needs to die, so he doesn't do this to someone else. Because I wouldn't be surprised if Leo strung along another woman somewhere. An unexpecting little lady with a bit of cash on hand he'd be willing to sweet-talk her out of."

Reaching out of his bedroll, he found her hand and squeezed it, loving the touch of her skin. "Really? Three women?" With a sigh, he said, "If he doesn't have one yet, he soon will."

"He's a dead man," Dora said quietly.

CHAPTER TWENTY-EIGHT

Without the children and the wagon, they rode from one town to the next searching for Leo and his magical miracle cure, trying not to succumb to the growing attraction between them. The fact they no longer had three kids for chaperones didn't help any.

Dora did her best to keep Leo in her mind and how they were still man and wife, for better or worse. Couldn't get much worse than it was right now.

On the third day, they rode into Waco, Texas, and went to the law office.

When they walked in, Dora pulled out an old tintype she brought with her. "Good morning, Sheriff. My name is Dora Tennyson."

"Howdy, ma'am. What can I do for you?" he said. "I'm about to walk out the door."

"We're looking for this man," she said, showing the man the picture of Leo. "He's been going around to different towns selling his miracle cure, which killed Jesse's sister and almost me."

The sheriff jumped up. "How do you know him?"

"He's my husband," she said. "My estranged, supposedly dead husband."

Stunned at his response, Jesse stepped up. "He married Dora and also my sister. Seems the man doesn't understand bigamy is against the law."

The man sighed. "The reason I'm in such a hurry is because this man was here day before yesterday, selling his cure all. The Smyths bought the drink for their sickly son. This morning he passed away. I'm on my way to pick up the bottle from them and take their statements. The parents are devastated they lost their eleven-year-old boy."

Dora sank into a chair, despair overwhelming her, pain for the family gripping her. They were too late to spare a family a loved one. "We've been trying to warn as many people as we could. It appears the worst has happened. A child died from his miracle cure."

"What's in this stuff?"

With tears in her eyes, she let Jesse tell the sheriff the history of the fake liquid.

"My sister made the juice and drank it, but this last batch, Leo created by himself. Forty-eight hours later, she died from the drink. We think he may have used bad mushrooms. There is one family of mushrooms that is poisonous, and the good ones almost look identical. If you pick the wrong one, it will kill you."

The memory of being so ill came back to her. "I didn't even drink the stuff but put the cup up to my lips and that small amount made me sick," she said. "Jesse gave me charcoal and milk thistle. I don't know if the herbs are what saved me, but I'm still here," she said, gazing at the sheriff.

"Do you think it would help if we spoke to the family?" Jesse asked.

The older man shook his head. "Not a good idea. They want his blood. Of course, I do too."

"We all do," Jesse said. "That's why we're trying to catch him."

A smile spread across Dora's face. "Sheriff, we need an arrest warrant for him. Besides being his wife, I'm a bounty hunter. I'll make certain he comes to your jail."

As much as she hated the fact a child was killed, she was determined the boy's death wouldn't be in vain.

The man nodded. "Why don't you meet me back here at two o'clock? I'll talk to the family and see if I have enough to convict him of murder. Get the bottle and see what else I can learn. If there is enough evidence, which I think there will be, I'll write you an arrest warrant."

A giddiness filled Dora as she stood and faced the man and held out her hand. "Thank you. Thank you for taking action. We've been warning people but felt like we weren't getting anywhere. Leo even tried to have me murdered, but the sheriff did nothing."

Sometimes the law was a little slow to act, but finally it seemed they had everything they needed to arrest Leo, once they found him.

"That Smyth boy didn't deserve to die this way."

"No, sir, a child is supposed to be protected from people like Leo. We'll bring him back to you as soon as we can," she promised, hoping she could deliver on that deal.

Jesse shook the man's hand. "Thank you, Sheriff. My sister's babies didn't deserve to lose their mother. Now I'm their caretaker because I refuse to let them go to their father."

The man smiled and Jesse and Dora walked out of the building and hugged one another in the street. "The law is finally getting on our side. Now we need to find him."

CHAPTER TWENTY-NINE

Still no arrest warrant. Still no wanted poster. The sheriff in Waco determined he didn't have enough evidence to convict Leo of murder. Even though he believed he did kill the eleven-year-old boy. Disappointment rode them hard as they left town. At least, he didn't close the investigation, but rather told them to bring him in. He wanted to talk to him.

But that would not be easy.

Two more days of traveling from town to town, trying to find Leo kept Jesse and Dora on the road. In Roundrock, they learned he was headed to Austin and they hurried to reach the bustling city.

Late in the afternoon, they arrived in the town, and for the first time in a week, decided to stay at a hotel. Only problem-- they had one room left with a full-size bed.

For a moment, they stared at one another before Dora spoke up. "We'll take the room. Make certain you send up hot water for a bath."

Before she could respond to the clerk, Jesse paid for the room, giving her a glance to remind her it was his turn. How was he going to sleep with her in the same room, the same bed, sharing the same bathtub?

Once they were settled in the room, a manservant brought up two buckets of steaming water and a tub. While Dora took a bath, Jesse had to get out of the hotel room. He couldn't stay with her naked, bathing behind a screen. All he could think about was kissing her sweet luscious mouth, pulling her against him and caressing her firm breasts. So he escaped the room.

With a sigh, he walked the streets of Austin hoping and praying he would see Leo selling his goods and take him out right then. But he found nothing. Maybe he had gone on to San Antonio. Maybe he returned to the farm, but wherever Leo was, he hoped he stayed away from his children. They were Jesse's main concern.

As he walked, he noticed the sights and smells, the call of the vendors on the street, the rush of a horse and buggy as they pulled people to their destinations. Soon this would all come to an end. Every day they got closer, and when this was over, he and Dora would never see each other again.

The idea troubled him. The woman was everything he ever dreamed of having in a wife, except for one major problem. Her inability to have children. And he wanted his own family so terribly bad. Could he give that up for a woman? Would he come to regret his decision?

The thought of the three faces waiting for him in Dallas overwhelmed him. Why did he want more kids when he had a ready-made family?

Yet, he dreamed of his wife and him experiencing their first child and then the second and third. His sons and daughters maturing into adults and the wishes he hoped for them. An old man with grandchildren bouncing on his knee. Could he give that up for Dora?

How did he know? Because of her wedding vows, they barely

kissed. Yet he respected her for not cheating, though it left him hard and wanting.

With a quick turn, he headed toward the hotel. He didn't have any answers. Hopefully, clarity would come and he would receive the guidance he desperately wanted. At the moment, he wasn't certain. After all, his focus remained on finding Leo and making him pay for the killing of his sister.

When he stepped into the room, Dora stood dressed in a beautiful gown. "Wow, you look gorgeous."

"It's a dress I bought in Zenith to catch a new husband. Only as it was being finished, I learned there was no need for the new outfit. I'm still married."

"Let's go to dinner tonight. My treat. We're getting closer and, well, this will be our night."

With a saucy smile, she stepped to the door. "I'll be waiting for you downstairs. Don't make me wait too long."

The moment the door closed, he shucked his clothes as fast as possible, stepping into the hot water and scouring his dirty body. What would they do tonight about the bed situation? Somehow the idea of sleeping on the floor was not ideal, but then again, how did he sleep beside her without touching her?

In a matter of minutes, he bathed, shaved, and put on a clean pair of clothes. When he entered the lounge area of the hotel, he saw a man sat talking to Dora. Jealously surged through him, his stomach cringed at the sight of the man. Who was this?

"Jesse," she said, standing and the man rose as well. "This is the lieutenant governor of Texas and he told me where the sheriff's office is located."

"Thank you," he said, thinking the man would like the opportunity to show her a lot more if he hadn't shown up. How could he feel jealous when he knew she would never go against her wedding vows and the woman was very much married.

"Folks, have a lovely evening. I recommended the Rose Cafe to your wife."

His wife? She told him they were married? Why?

"Again, thank you and nice to meet you."

The man walked away and Jesse held out his arm. "Shall we?"

"Don't you look handsome tonight," she said, smiling.

"Thank you, dear wife," he said, teasing her.

"The man assumed we were together, because I didn't tell him anything."

"Didn't bother me," he said, looking down at her and thinking she would be so perfect. What the hell was the matter with him?

"We haven't had any fun in a long time. Let's enjoy tonight and not think about Leo or the poison or even the children. Let's make this about you and me having dinner together. Very soon, we'll part ways and it would be nice to have a few pleasant memories of a good time with you."

A grin spread across his face. The woman had an uncanny way of reading his mind. That was exactly what he wanted of tonight as well. "Where is this Rose Cafe?"

"The cafe is a block down this road. When we turn right, the restaurant should be there on the corner."

The wind blew her loose blonde curls and the urge to brush them away from her face consumed him, but he resisted. Instead, he placed her hand in the crook of his arm as they walked down the sidewalk. "These last few days is the first time we've been alone together."

"Yes," he said, thinking how difficult it had been to lie beside her each night, knowing he couldn't touch her. Before the children chaperoned them, but now, only her vows kept them apart.

Once they reached the restaurant, they were promptly seated.

"Look, we're not eating while sitting on the ground in front of a fire," she said softly. "This feels so good."

Yet, this was way harder than eating out under the stars. Here, people surrounded them as Jesse stared across the table at her. Tonight, Dora looked stunning with her curls down her shoulder. The bodice of her dress fit snug against her breasts and all he could think about was how much he longed to take her back to the hotel room.

That would be crazy. Especially since she could not give him what he wanted. And yet, his heart and even his soul reached out to her, needing her, longing for her.

"Tell me something I don't know about you," she said, smiling and sending his pulse racing.

"My family you know all about. My sister, my nieces and nephew, and how I love to create things with wood," he stopped for a moment thinking what brought him pleasure.

A grin spread across his face as he raised his head. "Fishing is my favorite thing to do in the whole world. Just got back from a trip down to Galveston where I almost bought a boat and didn't return. But something told me not yet and here I am. Came home and found that Leo had left."

Like the slamming of a jail cell, he stopped himself from saying anything else. Tonight, they weren't going to talk about Leo and the havoc he created in their lives.

"Now it's your turn," he said.

Shaking her head, she laughed. "I'm the youngest of four children. The others all moved away and left me alone with my father after my mother died. There is a twelve-year difference between me and the oldest."

A sigh escaped and she picked up her water glass. "On my twelfth birthday, after a cyclone tore up our home, we left Kansas. My papa decided he'd had enough, so we came to Texas."

The baby of the family, he couldn't imagine. The oldest, he grew up quickly to take care of Ida.

"What did you do when you were a kid?" he asked.

"Played with my sisters and brothers, with my dolls," she said. "As the baby, I was all girly girl."

"After you told me you had been to that bounty hunter school,

I thought what a waste of time and money. Until I saw you pull your pistol."

The waitress brought out their dinner and set it on the table in front of them. Staring at the steaks and potatoes, he didn't know who he was hungrier for, the food or Dora.

They began to eat, both digging into the grilled steak. Tonight was the first really good meal they had shared since they left Gainesville.

"Ruby and her sisters learned from their father and now they teach others how to be a bounty hunter."

"You must have been their star pupil," he said, thinking never had he seen anyone draw that fast.

"Maybe."

Later, strolling down the sidewalk, the street noises soothed him as she held onto his arm. The sound of horses' hooves against the brick streets and music from a saloon echoed down the avenue.

"Tonight was wonderful," she said, gazing up at him. "Years have passed since I enjoyed myself so."

He nodded, thinking he had no idea when he would experience such an evening again. Once they located Leo and he returned to the children, his life would be wrapped around raising the kids.

"Do you ever wish your life was different," she asked.

"All the time," he said. "All my life I've wanted to live on a boat on the ocean. That we lived on the water and I swam and fished every day."

"Soon fishing would become a habit and not a pleasure," she said.

"What about you?" he asked, slowing them, not wanting to reach the hotel.

"If I had been the oldest and not the baby, then Papa would not have rushed me to marry and leave," she said. "If I were the oldest, I would never have married Leo."

Jesse nodded. "Then I would never have met you and we would not be chasing him."

"True, but my life would be happier. Who knows, I might even have children."

They were back to the wooden beam lodged between them. Yes, he wanted a family, a son of his own and she was barren.

"We're here," she said, glancing up at the hotel. There was no way he would stay while she undressed or be lost to the desire rumbling inside him.

"This has been a lovely evening," she said.

"Yes, it has. We both understand that we must be careful or tonight could turn into disaster," he said, unable to tell her that yes, he wanted to sleep with her, but knew it was impossible.

"What if I go up first and prepare for bed, then when you come in. I'll be in bed waiting with a bed roll between us," she said, gazing at him with such longing in her eyes, it was almost his undoing.

Would a bedroll really keep them separated?

"All right," he said, staring into her sapphire eyes, wanting to lose himself there. Dora turned to walk away when something inside him broke loose and he grabbed her.

Nothing could stop him as he pulled her to him, his mouth descending on hers. Her arms reaching up and sliding around his neck as he yanked her against him. Like a lost traveler, his lips moved over hers, saying what his heart and mind refused to acknowledge as he tasted her thoroughly, wishing with all his might this woman was his.

The sound of people walking along the street broke them apart.

Standing on the street, she stared at him in wonder. "No," she said softly. "No, we can't do this."

Like a frightened doe, she turned and fled into the hotel.

CHAPTER THIRTY

The next morning, Dora woke in bed with Jesse curled around her. Somehow during the night, he rolled over the bedroll onto her side and was snug up against her. How had this happened?

The feel of him lying next to her, his breathing assured her he slept, and her heart clenched with sadness. The night had been fun, and for just a little while, she pretended they were a happy couple out enjoying a meal together. But none of it was true.

Yet, last night was the closest to being courted she ever experienced. And Jesse was a man she would gladly give her love too. Lying here beside him, she wanted to roll over and take him in her arms and show him how he'd captured her heart.

A loving man who stood up for those he loved, and also knew the importance of family.

Yet, her wedding vows kept them apart and even her infertility. Once they apprehended Leo, she would disappear to nurse her wounded soul.

This morning, they would once again begin their search for her husband. With a sigh, she threw back the covers, jumped out of bed, grabbed her clothes and went behind the bathing screen.

"Good morning," Jesse called.

For some reason this morning, she felt frustrated. Yes, she wanted to catch Leo, but she also wanted her life to amount to something. Why couldn't she have a family? Children? Everything she wanted in life without having to give up Jesse.

"Good morning," she replied, trying to quell the tears that threatened to fall. Most of the time, she did all right with the realization she would never have children. Occasionally, all the disappointment would overwhelm her and send her into a major sinking spell that would take her days to recover. Right now, all the signals were showing one coming.

"You all right this morning?" he asked, his clothes rustling.

"I'm fine," she replied, knowing that wasn't true, but her sadness was none of his business. "What is the plan for the day?"

"Grab some breakfast, then talk to the sheriff," he said, and she heard him tugging on his boots.

After pulling her blonde hair up off her neck in a ponytail, she walked out from behind the screen and found him looking better than a man had a right to. What about Jesse, other than his way with children, his kind heart, and stunning handsomeness attracted her to him?

Could this attraction be because she knew he was off limits in her life at this moment? Or was she falling in love with him?

With a sigh, she realized the handsome cowboy who loved his family, who was a decent, honest man, she had fallen in love with. The realization was both happy and sad. Because though she loved him, she could never give him her heart. And she must never let him know.

She placed her night clothes into her saddle bags then picked up her toiletries and other items in the room.

"Want to stay another night?" he asked, his voice ruff.

Whirling toward him, she stared. "What? Why would we?"

"It's a great hotel," he said, moving to stand in front of her. "We could be here more than one night."

Suddenly, he placed his hands around her face and lifted her lips to meet his. The kiss was swift and firm, and her toes curled at the emotions he evoked. A rush of blood fired through her system, leaving her limp. She stepped back. "No, Jesse. You've got to stop kissing me."

"I like kissing you," he said, stepping closer to her.

The morning's thoughts slammed into her causing her to wilt.

"I'll never be able to give you the family you so desperately want. You deserve the children you long for. And me, who knows what's in store for me. But first we have a job to do. So let's go catch our bigamist killer so you can get back to the kids who need you."

With determination, she snapped her bag closed and started toward the door. Let the day begin and rid her mind of disappointments.

CHAPTER THIRTY-ONE

*J*esse stood beside Dora inside the Austin sheriff's office. "Have you seen this man?" she asked the sheriff, showing him the tintype.

For some reason today, she seemed on edge like last night had frightened her. The evening had been fun, relaxing, and when he entered the room, she'd feigned sleep.

Sometime during the night, he reached for her and this morning, when he awoke, she was in his arms, like she belonged there. Until he felt her jump out of bed.

Maybe she was as tempted by him as he was by her.

Until they captured Leo, he would not make any decisions regarding Dora. Right now, he had to concentrate on locating the man and his poisonous cure.

"No, ma'am, can't say I have," the sheriff said.

A deputy strolled through the office and the lawman called him over. "Daniel," he yelled, "take a look at this tintype. You ever seen this man?"

The man glanced at the picture. "Oh yeah, I know him. That's Leo Tennyson. He's been dating the spinster Ethel Green. We expect him to ask for her hand in marriage just any old day now."

The deputy gazed at them. "Why are you asking?"

Standing beside him, Dora tensed, the tension almost crackling aloud. "I'm married to him."

The deputy's mouth dropped open. "But Ethel thinks he's going to marry her."

An ugly laugh escaped Dora. "He might. She would be marriage number three. His second wife he killed with his miracle drink. Then he killed a child in Waco and a preacher's wife with his poison."

"Has he been peddling a drink called miracle cure on the streets?" the sheriff asked his deputy.

"Nope," he said, frowning. "And you're talking about Leo Tennyson?"

Jesse was ready to explode on the man. The law didn't care that he'd committed bigamy, or killed his sister, or that he was selling a poisonous concoction to unsuspecting people.

"Can you tell me where Ethel lives?" Dora asked. "I'd like to warn her. The man marries you, cleans out your bank account, and moves on."

"How long you been married to him," the sheriff asked.

"Ten years. Long enough to understand how he operates."

The two lawmen stared at one another and Jesse suddenly realized they didn't believe her. Sometimes the law could work against you.

"Spinster Green lives on Moss River Road. The mansion on the hill."

Dora turned and smiled at Jesse, both of them silently agreeing why the man was after the sprinter. If they hadn't come along, the lawmen would find the woman dead as soon as her bank account was transferred into his name.

"Thank you, gentlemen. Keep an eye out for him," Jesse said, taking Dora by the arm and leading her out the door.

The bright sunshine and a blast of warm air hit them as they stepped outside.

"Come on," he said as they hurried to their horses. He helped her on hers and then climbed on his own.

"We've got to warn her," Dora said, turning her horse and riding down the street.

And Jesse agreed, the woman needed to learn about Leo and his treacherous ways.

CHAPTER THIRTY-TWO

When they pulled up in front of the two-story stone mansion, Dora was shocked at the size of the huge home. Of course, Leo would like to date the woman. She obviously had money. Money he would gladly take from her. At the reminder of how he had stolen from her, anger burned in her gut like a smoldering fire.

They knocked on the door and a woman dressed in a maid's uniform answered. "May I help you?"

"We need to speak to Ethel Green," Jesse said. "It's important."

"Let me see if Miss Green is accepting visitors," she said and left them standing outside on the porch.

As Dora gazed at the property that ran along a river, she wondered how long the spinster had lived here.

The maid returned and gave them an irritated glare. "What is this about?"

"Tell her Mrs. Dora Tennyson, Leo Tennyson's wife, would like to talk to her."

In fewer than thirty seconds, the woman reappeared. "Follow me."

As they trailed the lady through the hallway, Dora noticed a shotgun standing next to the door. The woman led them into a formal parlor that held antiques with a mixture of modern wooden furniture. The place was immaculate with oil paintings and china bowls everywhere. While Dora's family had money, their wealth would never compare to this woman's.

"Come in," a woman older than Dora said, sitting like a regal queen in a chair in the fancy room. "Have a seat. Norma said you were Leo's wife. I don't believe you."

Dora pulled out the tintype. "This is my husband Leo Tennyson. Five years ago, I received a telegram saying he had been killed. When I went to the bank, my account had been cleaned out. Then several months ago, he was seen in Fort Worth, selling his miracle cure."

The woman's eyes narrowed as she stared at the picture.

Jesse sighed. "My sister married Leo five years later. Together they have two children. Last month, she died after drinking Leo's miracle cure. Leaving me to raise Leo's kids."

The woman frowned, her lip snarling.

"Children? There must be a mistake. Leo never mentioned any children. This is hard to believe. His wealthy family came from Boston. Maybe you have him confused with another Leo. With our money joined, we would be millionaires."

"There is no family in Boston, and he is broke," Dora said, knowing this had to be a total shock to the woman, who probably only wanted someone in her life.

She frowned. "I loaned him a thousand dollars because the bank was having trouble wiring his funds to him." Shaking her head, she closed her eyes, her mouth thinning into a straight line. "How can I believe you?"

The woman was tough, but Dora wasn't done yet. "The marriage records can be verified at the county courthouse in Zenith, Texas, ten years ago."

"Ten years ago? Good Lord, and you don't have children?"

Dora felt her insides clench. Why did it always come back to her weakness?

"No, children," she said softly. She tried to smile, but Dora's mouth just wouldn't work.

"My sister and Leo married in Gainesville almost six years ago. You could get a detective to verify this information."

The woman's features were stark and not very pretty. "Wait a minute, didn't you say he took money from you?"

"Yes, inheritance from my family," Dora said, wondering why she would care.

"Why haven't you gone after him? Surely, his family could pay you back."

For a moment, she had to compose herself to keep from laughing out loud.

"I'm sorry. Leo's parents died in west Texas. He has no family in Boston. No one to pay his debts. Leo is as broke as a minister. Why do you think he made up this juice to sell that is responsible for three deaths? The man needs the cash. Now the law is looking for him, for killing an eleven-year-old boy."

Ethel's eyes narrowed. "No, he would never do something so vile. I'm having a hard time believing this. Leo showed me pictures of his family. And he's never sold any miracle cure here in town that I know of. The Leo I know would never lie and marry several women at once. That would be blasphemous. You need to leave."

Dora was ready to concede. If he harmed her, then that was her problem. They tried to warn her.

"Can you tell us when you expect him?"

Ethel all but hissed in her elegant gown. "No, I will not tell you anything else. Now go before I send Norma to fetch the sheriff."

Standing, Dora realized they wasted valuable time trying to caution her when she acted like they were the ones disrespecting her.

"We're going," Jesse said. "If you want to talk with us, we'll be in town and the sheriff knows how to find us."

The woman pulled back her shoulders and considered their words. "This is nonsense. My Leo would never do what you're saying. He would never marry more than one woman or steal her money."

At that point, the frustration from the day overwhelmed Dora. "For your sake, I hope not. I'd hate to see you lose this big fancy mansion because some con man cleaned your bank account out. Good day, Ethel, and best of luck in your new marriage."

Jesse slammed his hat on his head and followed Dora out the door. Of all the stuck up snobbery she'd ever experienced. The woman was too blinded by Leo's sweet talk to understand the damage he could inflict.

CHAPTER THIRTY-THREE

*J*esse dropped Dora off at the hotel and took their horses to the stable. He told her he had errands to run and he would soon return. Walking into their room, she stripped off her boots and lay across the bed gazing at the ceiling.

Through the open window, she heard horses and people traveling along the busy street. In the sterile room, loneliness overcame her.

Last night, she could not sleep with him next to her and today it seemed like everything overwhelmed her. Lying there in bed, she thought of her mother and father, her brothers and sister, and even Leo. All the people she once loved came to mind and then she pictured Jesse and her heart shattered.

Yes, she'd fallen in love with the man, but they would never work for so many reasons. Mainly, he wanted a family and her womb was as empty as a church on Monday morning. Barren. The word was ugly and cold and filled her with such intense emotions of loss and sorrow.

It was like someone you dreamed of, but had never met, died. Like a part of you shriveled up inside. With Leo, she had come to accept they would never have children, but she believed life had given her a second chance, only to learn Leo had babies.

While she would never wish this on any woman, the fact Ida bore Leo babies hurt in the worst way.

And now all her fears were confirmed. Never would she feel a baby kick inside her or hold her child in her arms. Never would she gaze at her children and think they looked like her mother or father or her husband. Never would she see a child of hers grow into adulthood, marry, and give her grandchildren.

Being infertile was a life sentence. Eighty years without a family.

Jesse, the man she'd fallen in love with, dreamed of having his own family. Her heart ached with a sadness that tore her apart. While she would never have her dreams, Jesse deserved his.

A son to carry on his name, a daughter who would call him daddy. How could she ever wed any man again? Let alone a good, honest, kind-hearted man like Jesse.

Pain clenched her insides as the despair overwhelmed her. Tears spilled down her cheeks, and she curled up in a ball and cried herself to sleep.

CHAPTER THIRTY-FOUR

*D*ora had not been herself all day and he didn't know what was wrong, but after this afternoon, they both needed some fun. So he went to the store and purchased items for a picnic.

With the sun setting, he knew the time was too late to take her to a park, but they could have one in the room. After buying the food, he also bought a bottle of whiskey and playing cards. Something to take her mind off Leo and whatever troubled her.

How it must hurt a woman to learn her husband not only cheated with one woman, but now beguiled another one. While he didn't think she loved Leo any longer, the man had taken so much from her.

Time to cheer her up and bring back the spunky, fun-loving woman he grew fonder of each day. The woman who if only she could bear him children, he'd be all over her like a bee on honey.

Maybe it was wrong, but he longed for his own son and daughter. In fact, he wanted a whole passel of kids to chase around the house, the yard, and play with their mother.

Opening the hotel room door, he saw Dora sit straight up in bed. She'd been napping.

"Looks like someone was sleeping. Did I keep you awake last night?"

It was then he noticed the tear stains on her cheeks.

"No," she said, wiping her face.

How did he handle this strong woman breaking down in tears? Before he could make his decision, she rose from the bed and acted like nothing was wrong. "What did you get?"

Walking in, he held up the basket. "A picnic."

Turning, she gazed outside. "It's a little dark for us to go to the park."

A grin spread across his face. "True, but we could have one right here in the room."

Anything to cheer her up and wipe the sadness from her face. "What else?"

Staring at her, he laughed. "You're awfully curious."

"Get on with it, I'm hungry," she said, her voice trembling. "It's been awhile since breakfast."

"Well, after today, we needed some fun tonight. That Ethel was a character."

"More like a bitch, if you ask me," she said.

Since he met her, Dora had always been a woman who let him know how she felt, but the words were a little harsh even for her. Yet, he could see the pain on her face and knew she spent the afternoon crying. For her sake, he would be glad when this was over.

"That's more like my girl," he said, trying to be cheerful. "Well, I bought us a bottle of whiskey, because I never drink in front of the kids and I longed for a little adult refreshment."

"What if I don't like alcohol," she said.

Most women didn't like the taste and he couldn't argue with them. The liquor was strong, but the whiskey certainly went down easy and sometimes it helped him relax. They both needed to calm down and for one night forget about this frustrating hunt. When they found Leo, they would need their wits about them.

"I'm sure you won't be offended by me taking a little sip."

He walked into the room and sat everything on a table. "Also, I bought a deck of cards. Instead of sitting around moping tonight, I'm going to teach you the fine art of playing poker."

"Too late," she said. "My father taught me."

"Oh, he did," he said. "Good, then you won't mind me taking some of your hard-earned cash."

"You ain't getting a dime," she said.

"Strip poker?"

"Oh no," she said turning to the food. "Where's the whiskey?"

Well, that was certainly not what he expected to hear. Reaching into his shirt, he pulled out the small bottle of liquor.

"Do we have glasses?"

After he found two, he carried them to the table where he opened the bottle and poured them each a small amount and then lifted his glass. "To Leo. May he soon land behind bars and spend the rest of his life there."

They clinked their glasses together and he watched as she took a chug of the drink. With a gasp, her eyes widened, and tears formed in her eyes. The woman had never tasted whiskey.

"Are you trying to poison me?" she choked.

"No," he said, laughing. "This stuff is great whiskey."

Shocked, she poured herself another half glass and lifted her cup to his. "To Leo. May a bullet with his name etched on the metal find its way into his chest."

Once again, they clinked their glasses and she downed a second glass. This time, she handled the liquor a little better.

"We need to eat. That alcohol is going to hit you and you're going to be drunk soon."

The idea of her hanging her head over the slop jar or passing out from the alcohol was not something he wanted to experience.

"I've never been drunk in my life," she said, sitting at the table as he opened the dishes of food. "What did you bring us?"

"A couple pieces of cold chicken, potato salad, and apple pie." Her eyes lit up and a warmth rushed through him.

When she was happy, she was such a beautiful, exciting woman. Whatever happened that made her upset today, he hoped this would cheer her up. With everything Leo put her through, she deserved some happiness. She warranted a man who would love and care for her. And Jesse wanted her.

"I'm starving."

In a matter of moments, they finished the dinner Jesse had brought. After dropping her chicken bones, she wiped her hands and moaned. "Thank you for doing this."

"I thought we should have a picnic since you needed some cheering up today."

"Was it that obvious?" she asked, her face questioning. "Everything sort of came crashing down on me this afternoon. First the sheriff's total disregard for the fact Leo had married two women and was about to marry a third. And Ethel not believing that Leo would do something so egregious. Are women that crazy over men?"

In some ways, she was such an innocent as he busted out laughing, wiping his hands. "Some are. Never seems to happen to me, but yes, some take a look at a man and go all nuts over him."

Twirling the empty glass in her hand, she shook her head.

"For years, I wondered what my father saw in Leo that he would push me toward him. I can't answer that question. Papa made it clear I should marry him."

With a sigh, she set down her empty cup. "So, I married Leo thinking this was what I was meant to do, only to learn very quickly my husband was an impatient man. Someone I never seemed to make happy."

Jesse sighed and remembered his sister saying almost the same words. "Ida said the same thing to me, so you weren't the only one who found him difficult. That she didn't know what he wanted, but whatever she did, it was not enough. Maybe no woman will ever make Leo happy. There is something he's searching for and women are just stepping stones on his journey to find what he wants."

"Money?"

Oh yes, that was exactly what he meant. Leo had dollar signs in his eyes, selling poisonous drink, marrying ladies with cash and stealing. Never working a day, but rather trying to con his way through life.

"Like wealth and riches, which will never make him content," Jesse said.

While they sat eating their apple pie, she asked, "We still playing cards?"

"Oh yes," Jesse said. "The plan is to show you what a smart poker player I am."

"What are we betting on? No, don't say Leo because I won the shooting contest. Don't forget, I'm the one who is going to kill him."

"Don't get your hopes set too high on that one," he said.

Pouring them yet another drink, he gazed at her in amazement as she lifted her cup. "May the best person for the job shoot him. Me."

He laughed and clinked his against hers as he took a sip while she downed the entire glass. Pouring her more whiskey, he lifted his glass. "May my bullet find him first."

"If we keep doing this all night, trying to outdo the other, we're going to be mighty drunk. Bad things happen when people have too much to drink," she said, gazing at him. "You are one handsome man. And your lips feel really good against mine. Remember, I'm no longer a widow."

As he stared across the table, her full mouth beckoned him,

and he wanted to growl. If she wasn't careful, she would be experiencing his lips again. Something had to give before he had her naked in bed.

"Let's play cards before you pass out."

"Don't worry, I'm not going to pass out," she said. "By golly, if I can survive Leo's miracle cure, I can withstand whiskey."

Famous last words spoken by a drunk. Leaning toward her, he whispered, "Remember, I saw you naked."

"How can I forget," she responded softly. "But being ill is not the way to see a woman. My memory recalls, I was throwing up and other ghastly things a nice person doesn't discuss."

Still the woman's curves were in all the right places, her shapely hips and full breasts were something he dreamed about. "Everything looked pretty spectacular to me."

"I bet I look better now," she said softly. "Especially since I'm not sick."

Did the woman realize what a temptation she was? Did she realize every night it was all he could do not to ravish her while they shared the same bed? Did she realize he was in a constant state of arousal because of her nearness?

"Dora, unless you want me crossing the line, stop. In the morning, you would hate the fact your vows were broken because we got drunk and things went too far. Deal the damn cards before you find yourself naked in that bed."

Laughing, she grabbed the deck and began to shuffle. As she leaned back and dealt the hand, she sighed softly. "Why are you such a good, tempting man? But you're right. Leo doesn't deserve my loyalty, but I made a pledge before God I would not cheat and I'm sticking to that vow."

Not saying anything, he watched her, making up his mind. The temptation was too much and too soon, he would not act on his desires.

"Seven card stud it is. Once this is over, we're going to talk."

"No, once this is over, the talking is done. We're going to have sex," Jesse said, staring at her as her mouth dropped open. "Hot, raunchy, loving sex. Be prepared."

With a toss of her blonde hair, her brows raised in a question.

"Then, by golly, my bullet is the one that will take him down."

"Woman, you have to have the last word," he said almost growling. "Deal the cards or I'm taking you to bed right now."

A grin spread across her face as she dealt them each a hand.

An hour later, Jesse held her blonde hair as she barfed into the slop jar.

"Were you trying to kill me?" she asked.

Shaking his head, he glanced down at his dusty boots with colorful puke on them.

"Don't tempt me."

"I've never had hard liquor."

"Really?" he said sarcastically. "At least last time you were naked when you were throwing up."

She glanced up and glared at him. "Thanks for reminding me."

He shrugged. "Honey, you look gorgeous no matter what you're doing. Though I must admit, I like you better when you're all curled up next to me."

Dora moaned as she retched again.

The memory of all those luscious curves now hidden made him groan. What was it with this woman? She left him hard and wanting and dreaming of the two of them between the sheets.

CHAPTER THIRTY-FIVE

The next morning, Dora sat over a cup of coffee, her head pounding. What possessed her to drink so much whiskey? Sadness.

Today, she kept the demons at bay, though she knew as soon as this was over, for Jesse's sake, she would leave.

Even last night, his comments regarding them having sex made her smile at the thought. Dora loved this man. Probably had fallen in love with him before they left Gainesville. There was no way they could ever be together.

"You all right this morning?" he asked. "You look a mite peaked."

Lifting her eyes to his, she gave him a painful stare. The light from the window was like an arrow piercing her skull. "Fine."

"Would you tell me if you weren't?" he asked, grinning.

Hell would become a sanctuary for angels before she would admit to him how the alcohol left her queasy, her head pounding.

"This morning, I feel like a new Georgia peach. Sweet and delicious."

"Liar," he said. "You've been staring at your coffee cup for ten minutes.

"I'm savoring the liquid," she said, thinking she didn't know if her stomach would revolt. Never again would she partake of whiskey. Never again would she drink until Jesse put her to bed. This morning, she awoke in her chemise and pantaloons. At least he hadn't taken all her clothes off.

"Well, savor a little faster. We need to stake out the widow's house before Leo shows up," Jesse said.

"Maybe we should wait until tomorrow," she said, wondering if the alcohol affected her aim. Missing her target, especially a man she had waited so long to kill, would be devastating. A man who had taken everything from her.

The glance Jesse sent warned her they couldn't stay in this room any longer. "Eat your breakfast."

A quick gaze at the eggs let her know they were still there. Still waiting for her to take a bite. "You're treating me like a child."

A laugh erupted from him. "That's because you're acting like one. You're acting like Ella when she doesn't want to eat. If she doesn't like the food, she ignores it, hoping it will magically disappear."

For a moment, Dora closed her eyes as the image of Ella appeared, and Ben, and even Grace. All three and she knew for their safety, she had to gather her strength. "Just remember, I'm never drinking with you again."

A grin spread across his face. "Never is a long time."

"Well, it's true," she said, taking a bite of her eggs. They didn't taste too bad. In fact, her stomach growled loudly.

"See, you were needing food," he said.

"A gentleman does not draw people's attention to the sound of a woman's stomach," she chastised as she took another bite.

"Yes, we have so much company," he said with a laugh.

In fewer than five minutes, she pushed back from the table. Already the effects of the alcohol were less.

"Now we're going to Ethel's house?"

"Yes, and don't forget to bring your canteen. The day is going to be long and hot."

Sitting outside in the heat with her stomach queasy, her head pounding, sounded like a disastrous way to spend the afternoon.

What possessed her to drink so much? The overwhelming depression she felt yesterday. Some days it overpowered and dragged her down. After visiting with Ethel, she left feeling beaten.

"Does she have an outhouse?"

His brows drew together. "I think so."

"Good, I may need to use it," she said. "I detest going in the bushes."

A grin spread across his face. "Come on, let's get going."

While Jesse went to the stable to procure their horses, Dora waited outside the hotel. Standing on the corner, she saw a man dressed in a suit, who looked like Leo hurrying down the main street. No way she could be so lucky.

Stunned, she hurried after the figure, hoping to identify the man. The suited man disappeared into a jewelry store. When she caught up, she peered through the window as Leo looked at the wedding rings and finally chose the cheapest one.

Disbelief filled her at the audacity of the man and the urge to run in and shoot him almost overwhelmed her, but this wasn't the time.

Trying to act nonchalant, but get close to the window, she heard the clerk laughing. "Are you going to ask her."

"This afternoon," Leo responded. "Need to finish up some business this morning, and this evening, I'm taking her to dinner."

As he paid for the ring, Dora turned and all but ran down the street back to where she waited for Jesse. Should she tell him what she learned? Or should she keep this information to herself. Soon, this would be over. Soon, she would kill Leo and move on with her life.

Thirty minutes later, they were riding toward Ethel's house, their horses making clip-clopping noises along the dry dusty road. "Did you find Ethel attractive?" she asked.

Shaking his head, he laughed. "Not especially. Sure, she was a pretty woman at one time, but I never was attracted to mean redheads."

"Yes," Dora said. "Redheads can be a bit touchy," she said, thinking of Meg who owned the dress shop in Zenith. The woman was her friend, but she never wanted to cross her or find herself on her bad side.

They rode along in silence until Dora asked, "Where are we going to hide?" She cocked her head, thinking. "Somehow, we need a view of him riding up the road. There are the woods on the side of the house. What about there?

"We would see him walking up to the house, and before he entered, kill him and take his body to the sheriff."

"All right, but we're going to capture him, not kill him," he said, not looking at her.

She gave him a glare that clearly told him what she thought of that idea. "Why are you so determined to turn him in? Have you forgotten he killed your sister?"

The man kept teetering back and forth between taking him in and killing him. After everything he'd done, he had to die.

"Because three children are waiting for me to return," he said. "I'm not going to murder anyone."

Always the practical one, when she would just like to end the man's evil.

"So, we're going to hide in the woods on the side of the house. He's going to run as soon as he sees us," she said.

Jesse frowned. His horse made a snorting noise as a fly buzzed him. "Probably. I'll be ready in case he tries to get away."

An eerie sense of foreboding overcame her. Like they were riding toward trouble instead of stopping chaos from happening.

As they neared the home, she faced him. "Why don't we hide

in those bushes near the house? There's plenty of cover. Let's leave our horses tied up in the woods."

"Sounds good," Jesse said.

In a comfortable hideout, not far from the house, they spent the next few hours, watching the comings and goings of the mansion. All afternoon, Dora waited, hoping somehow she could ditch Jesse before Leo arrived.

This was her chance, her opportunity, and she planned on taking advantage of the skills she learned in bounty hunting school. After all, that was what would keep her from starving after this was over.

"Wait here," Jesse said. "I've got to use their outhouse. Hopefully, nothing will happen while I'm gone."

"Sure," Dora said, smiling, knowing her chance was at hand. After a minute, she followed Jesse, picking up a broken limb. The door closed behind him and she lifted the stout branch to place it against the door, effectively jamming the handle.

Jesse rattled the door. "What the hell?"

"Sorry, Jesse I've got to do this on my own. Talk to you soon."

Loud cursing filled the air and she hoped the door held while she hurried back to the house. Once again, she hid in the bushes, waiting. Before long, Leo appeared driving his wagon up the street to the spinster Ethel's house.

Dora took a deep breath and steadied her nerves. For months, she'd been anticipating this showdown. The man was about to die.

CHAPTER THIRTY-SIX

The woman had locked him in a stinking outhouse in July. A place where the flies and yellow jackets loved hiding out. A place where even the snakes liked to hide from the hot Texas sun.

"Dora," he screamed, not caring that the spinster might find him. Better to face her than die in here of heat exposure or of the stench. No response to his yelling.

He hit the door. It wouldn't budge. He slammed his back against the barrier and nothing happened. Sweat started to bead up on his neck and face, his breathing labored.

The woman would be in so much trouble when he found her. Running his hand along the boards, he noticed several in the back were loose. Leaning back, he kicked the wall of the structure and saw the first rays of daylight. Thirty minutes later, after struggling, he managed to kick the last board that would free him.

Fresh air overwhelmed him as he climbed out of the dark, stinky building and blinked in the sudden sunlight. For a moment, he stood still, his ears picking up the sound of voices.

Dora and Leo.

He could hear the two arguing from the front of the house. The blast of a gunshot echoed through the late afternoon, sending the birds in the trees fluttering into the sky.

Fear spiraled through him and he ran as fast as his tired, sore legs would run. Dora needed him.

If something happened to her... His heart pounded in his chest and he pushed himself harder.

CHAPTER THIRTY-SEVEN

Dora stepped out of the bushes directly into the path Leo walked. He stopped and stared at her, a grimace on his face.

"Do you have a death wish?" he asked her. "I've already warned you once not to follow me."

She flicked the strap on her guns, her eyes never leaving his. "You're supposed to be dead."

"If you hadn't found me, I could still be dead," he said.

"The sheriff of Zenith saw you in Fort Worth selling your miracle cure," she responded, her feet moving to her shooting stance, ready to end his life now. All Leo had to do was try to stop her and her guns would come out flying.

All the years they were married flashed before her eyes. From the time they said I do to the moment she received the telegram. The ups and downs, the fights, even the good times. All those years wasted on a man who didn't love her.

"I hoped he hadn't seen me that day."

"So, did you marry Ida before or after your death?" Why she asked, she didn't know. She wanted to understand why he would leave her destitute.

"Now, Dora, honey," he said, walking toward her, using the voice he used to kiss and make up. Like hell.

"Stop," she commanded. "I'm not your honey, so don't pretend that I don't know what you're doing. Today, you bought a ring and you're here to propose to Spinster Ethel. Eventually you would do the same thing to her. How many women have you married, stolen their money, and then left? How many? For some reason, I don't think I'm the first."

A laugh resounded from him. "Honey, you make me sound bad. After I figured out we would never have children, I decided it was time to find someone who could give me some kids. Your inheritance was the down payment on a new life with Ida. And she gave me a daughter and a son."

Like a knife his words twisted in her heart, hitting her in the most vulnerable place.

With a gasp, she staggered a little at his admission. In the flash, he moved toward her and she pulled out her gun, the urge to kill him like an explosion inside her. "One more move and you're a dead man. Then, I'll sell the land."

With a sigh, he stopped. "So, you would sell the land meant for my babies and force them out of their home. My motherless children with only their uncle to care for them. You're as much a monster as I am. At least, I just con women. You harm children. No wonder you're barren."

Appalled, hate filled her and she raised her pistol, determined she would end this misery now. Like a poison, rage surged through her and she screamed. "It's time for you to die."

Bending over with laughter, he said, "You won't shoot me. I'm your husband and you believe in marriage."

Her determination faltered. "No, but I can arrest you."

"For what? Taking what became mine? For marrying someone who is now dead? What are you going to arrest me for?"

Her hand began to tremble and tears clogged her throat. The man was right. Though she hated him, a ring and those damn vows - for better or worse - got in the way. Plus, the law didn't seem to care he had done her dirty. They didn't care three people were dead because of him, but they would hang her for shooting him.

"Honey, we're married for better or worse, until death do we part," he said.

With a scream of outrage, she shoved her gun back in the holster and whirled around, so disappointed in herself. With her back to Leo, she heard the click of a gun. As she glanced up, she saw Ethel standing in the door facing her, holding her shotgun, and knew she was done.

Everything she'd fought for was for nothing, and in this moment, she would not live to see another day.

Ethel's gun fired and the slug whizzed by her ear and she thought the woman missed. A scream of pain and agony had her whirling around. Leo lay on the ground writhing, a gun not far from his hand. Ethel came down the steps carrying her shotgun and kicked the gun away from him.

"You lying, cheating, scoundrel. Her money is the last you'll ever steal. Rest in hell," she said, spitting on him.

Stunned, Dora stood staring as her husband lay dying until Jesse came running around the corner, screaming her name. "Dora."

Once he reached her side, he grabbed her. "Are you all right?"

"I'm fine," she said, leaning into his side before she stepped away.

"I'm so angry at you. When the gunshot sounded, I feared you were hurt or worse, dying," he said, his face red, his brown eyes flashing with anger.

The man she loved had every right to be furious with her. What he didn't know was that Leo pointed a gun at her back and intended to kill her. If not for Ethel, she would be dead.

"Don't worry, I'm fine. Ethel shot Leo," she said as she watched the woman standing over Leo her gun pointed at him.

"Honest, Ethel, I was coming today to ask for your hand in marriage," Leo gasped.

"But you're married, and I don't take anybody's seconds," she said, her voice cold, her hand steady. "When we met, I told you that was my condition."

Turning, she gazed at Jesse and Dora. "Sheriff's on his way. My maid went to fetch him. I owe you an apology. After you visited me, I did some checking. I didn't know he was married."

Maybe the woman was a bitch, but she was a strong one who didn't take men and their crap, and Dora realized Ethel had saved her life.

"It's all right," Dora said, thinking she didn't want this woman mad at her. "How many other women did he deceive? If he had killed me, he would be free to marry you."

The woman made a growling noise. "No, I didn't want a scoundrel like Leo."

How would they ever know the depths of Leo's cheating? But at least now, his days of being a man who conned women and sold a poisonous concoction were over. Never again would Leo hurt her and yet, so many dangling threads to sort through. Threads Leo created and she couldn't walk away from.

Gazing at Jesse, a sadness came over her. Soon their time together would be over. And she missed him already.

CHAPTER THIRTY-EIGHT

Jesse's heart had been in his throat when he ran around the side of the house and saw Leo on the ground. Dora stood over Leo's body in shock with Ethel at her side holding a shotgun. He breathed a sigh of relief.

And yet, he was so angry at her for locking him in the outhouse. It had taken his rapidly beating heart a few minutes to slow down. Even then, he needed to walk away to control the tears that filled him at the thought of her being hurt.

Saddened, he realized their time together would soon come to a close and he didn't want it to end.

The sheriff arrived and took them one by one away to ask questions about what happened. The man was doing his job, and after today, this would be over. But what came next? Could he let Dora go? Could he ride away from her with the children?

And the kids...now he would tell them, not only had they lost their mother, but also their father.

With a sigh, he turned away and gazed down on the sidewalk at his hated brother-in-law. "You have my pledge with God as my witness, I'm going to raise my sister's children," he said. "Your babies will have a happy home."

Dead, the man didn't respond.

The lawman motioned him over. As he passed Dora, she whispered, "The sheriff thinks there's a love triangle."

Her message struck Jesse wrong and he started laughing. "He's going to be disappointed when he learns the truth."

She grinned and kept walking.

As he walked up to the man with the badge, he sighed. "You can't seem to stay out of trouble."

"What?" he asked, shocked at the man's statement.

He sent his deputies scrambling to find chairs and set them under the shade of a large oak tree. The lawman took his hat off and wiped the sweat from his brow. "Take a seat."

Jesse sat across from the man. "What kind of trouble are you referring to?"

"Yesterday you and Mrs. Tennyson sat in my office warning me about his poisonous miracle cure. Where is the poison?"

Stunned, Jesse leaned back. "It's not in his wagon?"

"Completely empty," the sheriff said. "Our community doesn't need a bunch of people dying from this tainted snake oil."

Did he believe they were going to sell the stuff?

"We need to locate that miracle cure," Jesse said, gazing at him. "Quickly or someone is going to die."

"Whoever he sold it to paid him enough cash he purchased the engagement ring for Spinster Green. So sometime between yesterday and today, he sold what remained of the miracle cure." The man sighed. "I'm going to let you and Mrs. Tennyson go on one condition."

"What's that?"

"Were you having an affair with Mrs. Tennyson?"

A smile crept across his face.

"Oh, Sheriff, I wish I could tell you yes. I'd be the happiest man alive if she would agree. Though Leo had multiple wives and didn't think a thing in the world about breaking his vows, Dora takes her vows very seriously. I won't lie and say I haven't tried, but she's told me no, she's a married woman."

Maybe he said too much. The man was frowning at him like he just made himself accessible to murder. If the man had been told the truth, he would know he'd been locked in the outhouse when Leo was shot.

The sheriff smiled. "Not anymore, she's not. Good thing the spinster confessed."

Still there was the poison. And it would give him that much longer with Dora.

"True, but now we've got to find that tainted water before whoever bought it dies."

The lawman spit out some chewing tobacco and sighed. "All of your stories match. You're free to go but find me the drink. You two would have a better idea on who he could have sold the miracle cure too. Locate the poison and destroy the drink."

The man sighed as he gazed at Jesse. "Get going. Before you leave, send out the spinster. I'm going to let her go, but I've got to at least warn her. Women can't go around shooting men, even if he was about to kill Dora."

Jesse froze. "What did you say?"

"According to Ethel, Mrs. Tennyson turned her back on Leo and was walking away. Leo would have shot her in the back if not for the spinster pulling the trigger. Appears she'd done some inquiries and learned what Dora told her the other day was the truth. Leo was married and had children."

Anger roiled through Jesse's veins. Yes, he took chances, but you never turned your back on a man with a gun. Never. Today, he almost lost Dora and the fact she locked him in the outhouse infuriated him.

CHAPTER THIRTY-NINE

"Let's go," Jesse called, his manner brusque.

Dora gazed at him and then glanced at the sheriff. What had the man said that riled him so? Because she knew the man well enough to recognize when he was thoroughly ticked off.

"Ethel, if the law gives you a hard time, we're staying at the Palmer Hotel downtown," Dora said, swinging her leg up and over her horse. Sitting in the saddle, the realization the hunt was over rattled her. Nothing held her here in Austin any longer. At any time, she could leave and begin her journey as a bounty hunter.

The idea didn't thrill her like she thought it would. In fact, she no longer wanted to chase bad guys. Leo had been enough and now she wanted nothing more than to return to her previous life.

"I'm not worried," the woman said. "If I hadn't killed him, he would have shot you," she said, and Dora wished she would've kept that little tidbit of information to herself. A look at Jesse and she could see the tightness around his lips.

"So long, Ethel," he called and spurred his horse.

Dora's mare fell into step with his. As they passed the wagon where Leo's body lay covered, she stared at him realizing for the first time she truly was a free woman. After ten long years, a widow and she felt no remorse.

Something bothered the man she loved.

Kicking the side of his horse, their speed increased.

"What's the big hurry?" she asked.

"The poison," he said. "It's missing."

"Oh no," she cried and eagerly followed him.

"The sheriff doesn't know what he did with the miracle cure," he said.

As they rode, Dora's mind went over the possibilities. Where did Leo find a buyer willing to give him cash for snake oil? Who would want poisoned drink? Not that they had learned the juice was deadly yet, but still.

"What if Leo sold it before he rode into town," she said out loud, her mind churning with possibilities. "Let's talk to the jeweler. Somehow he had the money to buy the ring, maybe he said something about who he sold the shipment to while buying the wedding band."

Jesse didn't know about her following Leo this morning.

Turning in his saddle, he glanced at her a questioning gaze on his face. "How did you know he went to a jeweler today?"

Licking her lips, there was no putting this off. She had to tell him the truth and hope it didn't make him any madder. "Because I saw Leo while you went for the horses this morning. I followed him to the jeweler down the street from the hotel where he bought a wedding ring for Ethel."

They rode along in silence and what she said only seemed to have fueled the blaze already burning within Jesse. The man's taut lip and the tick in his cheekbone clearly showed what she said made him angry.

"And you kept this information from me?"

There was no way to lie. "Well, yes. At the store, I overheard he planned to visit her this afternoon and I wanted to be the one to kill him."

"How did that work out for you?"

In all her training, she had never taken into consideration whether or not she could actually kill someone she knew. Even though she hated Leo and longed for him to be dead, in the end she could not pull the trigger. The reason wasn't lack of skill, rather her conscience stood in the way. Would it always be this way?

"Not well," she said softly. "You should have been there."

A tense silence came over them as they rode into the city.

"We're headed to the jeweler, but you're going to let me do the talking. You're going to let me do any shooting, and by golly, Dora the next time you lock me in an outhouse, you will find yourself across my knee. Do you understand?" He sighed. "The sheriff told me that Leo was going to shoot you in the back. I almost lost you today."

For a second, she sat there contemplating what he said, surprised at the venom in his voice.

He said, "What if Ethel had turned that gun on you instead of Leo?"

"Thank God, she didn't."

The memory of thinking that was exactly what was going to happen reverberated through Dora. "I'm sorry I locked you in the outhouse. Though I hated him, he was still my husband and a symbol of all my dreams.

"A happy marriage, kids, and someone to love me. How do you kill your dreams? At the last second, I couldn't. Right up until that final moment, I intended to shoot him."

His shoulders sagged. "Damn, you have this way of cooling my anger. For thirty minutes, I've been so mad at you for putting yourself in danger. And yet when you tell me why you couldn't kill him, I can't stay angry any longer. But, Dora, I'm warning you, no more outhouses. We do this together or not at all."

What were they doing together? Leo was dead. When they located the poison, they would part ways. Sure, she loved Jesse, but she also came to accept they would never be a couple. She loved him so much, she would walk away.

Besides, now that this was almost over, she would wander for a while. Bounty hunt when she needed money, then ride across the country and do whatever she desired. Knowing it would be an empty, lonely life.

While they were together, she wanted to make memories to carry with her, not dwell on her hollow future.

Riding side by side, she reached over and touched him on the arm. "The good news is I'm no longer married."

"Aargh," he growled. "That's what I'm talking about. One moment, I'm so angry with you, and now I want to ride as fast as we can to the hotel. But we can't."

A smile spread across her face. "Just trying to give you something positive to think about."

It was so easy to bedevil men and she loved the way she had Jesse in an uproar. These parting moments—she would enjoy every one of them.

"You're driving me absolutely crazy with want, woman. If you don't behave, I'm going to take you right here on the side of the road."

A giggle escaped. Last night while drinking, she believed his comment was the liquor talking, but he was serious.

"Never driven a man crazy with want. Kind of makes me feel special."

The glare he gave her should have singed her blonde hair, but instead she blew him a kiss. "We better hurry if we're going to reach the jeweler before closing. No time for stopping on the side of the road."

CHAPTER FORTY

The woman was exasperating and yet anticipation like a volcano ready to explode built inside him. How long had they waited?

It seemed like forever and he was past being subtle. He wanted Dora something fierce. Thank goodness the children were with his aunt.

As they walked into the jewelry store five minutes before closing, he hurried to the counter.

"Did Leo Tennyson come in here today to purchase an engagement ring," Jesse said.

"Oh yes, he is proposing to the spinster," the owner said. "The man's got a lot of courage to marry that woman."

The woman had bravely shot and killed Leo, but Jesse couldn't help but agree with the jeweler. "Did he mention his miracle cure and who he might have sold the drink too?"

The man thought for a moment. "Said he ran into a friend at the saloon last night who purchased his entire load. Roy..."

"What? He was in jail," Dora said. "How did he get out?"

The man laughed. "Easy. His brother is the sheriff of Fremont."

The look of fury on her face was almost comical, except lives were in danger.

Turning to Dora, Jesse said, "That's forty miles down the road."

"No," the jeweler said. "Leo saw him at the Colorado River saloon here in town."

It couldn't be coincidental the two men found themselves in Austin at the same time. And Leo sold the shipment to Roy?

He took a quick glance at Dora, and she said, "Let's go."

"Thank you so much. You've been a big help," he said, hurrying out the door.

In a matter of moments, they rode toward the saloon.

"Why would he purchase the miracle drink from Leo?" Dora asked as their horses trotted to the cantina.

The very same thoughts swirled through Jesse's head like a tornado churning the prairie, with no conclusion. None of this made sense. Had Leo pulled another con?

When they arrived at the saloon, they tied their horses and entered the darkened room. Not yet busy, they glanced around and found Roy drinking a beer.

They walked up to his table and he jumped and tried to run. "How the hell did you find me?"

"No wonder a wanted poster was never issued on Leo. I guess your brother, the sheriff, didn't want anyone pursuing his friend regardless that he killed three people," Dora said.

The way the law had helped Leo was unbelievable and yet what could she do?

The man glanced down at his almost full beer glass. "You got nothing on me."

"Oh attempted murder and rape is nothing?" she asked.

The man drank a sip of his beer. His hands were shaking and he looked pale even in the darkened saloon. "Where's the miracle cure?"

"I'm delivering it to a hospital in Houston. They're waiting on the juice and are going to give me a thousand dollars," he said, not looking at them.

"How much did you pay Leo for the wagon full?" Jesse asked, already seeing a swindle job.

"Five hundred dollars. I'll double my money when I reach Houston."

Leo's last con. Though something didn't seem right. Why would he still be sitting here? If he left today, he would be partway there by now. "So, you still have the wagon?"

"Yes, and you can't take it," he said his words slurring. Was the man drunk?

A frown crossed Dora's face. "Why aren't you on the road? That's a lot of money and I thought you'd be headed that way by now."

What would a hospital want with snake oil? Somehow Jesse knew the man had been lied to.

Roy closed his eyes, his head falling forward. "Leaving in the morning. They want to buy the balance of his stock."

The redness of his eyes, the way his hands were a blueish color alerted Jesse. "Did you drink any of the miracle cure?"

The man glanced up at him, his eyes pleading for help. "Yes."

"Didn't you hear us say it was poison? That a kid died?" Dora asked, frustration filling her. The man had been warned and yet he drank some anyway.

"Leo told me what you said was all lies and encouraged me to drink it to cure my joint pain," he whispered. "But I don't feel good."

Jesse shook his head. "Come on, man, we need to take you to a doctor. That stuff is poison and killed my sister. If we don't find you help, you'll soon be dead."

Roy tried to stand and started to fall as Jesse caught him. "Where's the wagon?"

"In the back," he said. "Promised me the miracle cure was great and I'd make my money back and then some."

Together, the two of them let him wrap his arm around their shoulders and they half carried, half dragged him out of the bar.

"Leo is dead," she said.

The man sighed. "Why do I keep following people like him? Twice this week he's gotten me in trouble and this time, I may die."

Jesse didn't say much knowing the man probably would perish.

"Mrs. Tennyson, I just want to apologize for what happened to you," he said.

If the man hadn't been dying, Jesse would have shown him how he accepted his apology. But the man was already turning that horrible blue tint and if he drank a full cup, there wouldn't be much they could do to help him.

"Apology accepted. Now does anyone else have any of this poison?"

As they reached the wagon, Jesse helped him inside and Roy sighed. "Not that I know, ma'am."

"Good," Dora said, tying Jesse's horse to the back. "We'll get you to a doctor and then we're going to destroy whatever's left."

"Once again, Leo took my money." Shaking his head, Roy leaned back against the seat. "We better hurry. I'm not feeling well."

Climbing up in the wagon, Jesse sat beside the man and clicked the reins to the horses. By the time they located the doctor's office, Roy had died.

CHAPTER FORTY-ONE

Sadness overwhelmed Dora as they walked into the hotel room. One last night together. One last night that had been marred by the death of Roy. One last victim of Leo.

Dropping her saddle bags on the floor, she sank down at the table where last night they had drank too much whiskey. The day seemed a thousand hours long. First with them waiting for Leo and then his shooting, the sheriff, and finding the poison.

The miracle cure was all drained from the bottles and they'd taken the empty glass and shown the lawman. Later, they sold the team and the wagon. Leo would no longer need them, and Jesse had a wagon and team for the children to ride in already.

"Is there any whiskey left? I think after today, I could use some."

"You said you were never going to drink again," he said, grinning at her.

"Today calls for a little liquor. A small sip, nothing more."

"Agreed," he said and found the nearly empty bottle. Just enough for them each to have a glass.

After he poured the liquor, she raised her drink to his. "To a great partner. To the end of my marriage and a new beginning in life."

A beginning she wasn't really sure she still wanted. With no family, she needed money to live on. So, a bounty hunting she would go.

In silence, they sat sipping their whiskey. The alcohol traveled down her throat, leaving a nice warm trail.

Standing, Jesse took her by the hand and she gazed up at him, questioning what he was doing. His hands wrapped around her head as he brought her lips to his and she knew. The man had not forgotten and fully intended to fulfill his promise from the night before.

Blood roared in Dora's ears as she leaned into Jesse's kiss, unable to resist the pull of his attraction any longer. The realization she loved this man left her feeling reckless. Consequences be damned, she was hungry for the sensation of his body twined with her limbs, delirious with wanting him, desperate to be possessed by Jesse.

The feel of his mouth plundering her lips as she returned his feverous kisses with a fierceness surprised her. Opening to receive him, she gripped his face and molded them together. The man tasted of sun-kissed days and pleasure-filled nights. Sweet, sinful sensations erupted in a delicious soft moan that escaped from deep inside her.

He gripped her shoulders as though he would never let her go, she relinquished all control as his lips consumed hers. Slowly he pushed her back until her legs bumped into the bed as he pressed his arousal through her skirts into the vee of her body.

From the touch of his muscular thighs to the strength of his sinewy chest, she felt all of him. Every delicious, rock-hard inch.

Sliding her hands down his shoulders, down his muscled back, past his waist, until she grabbed his buttocks, melding the two of them more firmly together. Five long years without a man. Five long years had passed since she experienced love, and tonight, she needed to soak up as much as possible, because this would be her last time forever.

Jesse moaned, his tongue tracing the ridges of her lips, his kiss turning savage as she held him against her, intoxicating her with desire. Nothing mattered at this moment except this man, this kiss, and the hardness of his body taut with need for her, only her.

The rational part of her mind refused to be quiet and warned her to step away. But it was too late to stop this crazy risk she was taking with Jesse. She was past the point of control. Nothing could keep her from being with this man.

This man made her stronger, made her do things she tried to resist, and for the first time in years, he made her feel like a woman.

His lips moved to her throat, pushing the soft fabric of her dress away as he slid his hands down the front of her bodice, skimming her curves like a man reading Braille.

"Are you certain about this," she said, tugging on his shirt, pulling the material free of his pants.

"Nothing could stop me," he whispered.

She wanted to touch his naked flesh, run her fingertips over his muscles, down the wisps of hair on his solid chest. She wanted to touch him, make him as giddy with passion as she was. She wanted Jesse, and she wanted him now.

The past be damned, the future was tomorrow, but tonight, she needed to experience the loving embrace of a man. Tired of fighting this thing between them, tired of denying the attraction for him and now there was no longer a reason to stop.

With a final tug, his shirt came free of his pants, and she slipped her hands inside, needing to touch his naked skin. Lightly she ran her fingertips along the hardened muscles of his chest, touching every solid ridge.

Why couldn't she put him out of her mind instead of craving his caress? With one smoldering glance, her senses quivered with anticipation. No man had ever intrigued her like Jesse.

"Dora," he moaned, his lips covering hers once more. Their kiss deepened as his fingers deftly worked at the buttons on the back of her dress until the sleeves slid over her shoulders, down her arms. The cool night air brushed her skin, and she experienced a moment of panic. What was she doing?

And then his mouth touched the sensuous part of her neck, causing her to shiver. His lips trailed past her neck, nipping the curvature of her shoulder. A shudder went through her as his mouth seared a path down her chest. With a final swish, her skirt landed in a pool around her feet.

At this moment, nothing else mattered but wanting Jesse. As her fingers fumbled with the buttons on his shirt, her breathing was fast, her pulse pounding. Clumsily, she undid each button, resisting the urge to stop and explore his body.

As she undid the last button, she yanked the garment off his back and tossed it to the floor with the other clothes. A tremor of need ran through her as she reached for the buttons on his pants.

There were no promises for tomorrow. There were no declarations of love, though he had captured her heart. There was only this need to experience his arms around her and be loved.

"Wait, Dora," he whispered, as he tugged his boots off, kicking them across the room as he stood, and she leaned into him and kissed his naked flesh. Gently running her tongue along his chest, his skin rippling from the effect.

He grabbed her shoulders and pushed her back. Quickly he untied the front of her chemise and pulled the cotton garment over her head, throwing the material in a haphazard way. Bare from the waist up she stood before him.

She stopped and kissed Jesse, leaning into his embrace, unable to bear their bodies being separated. Her lips expressed what her heart knew and her voice could not say as he pulled the string on her drawers.

They dropped to her feet, leaving her naked and exposed. With a kick, she stepped out of her pantaloons. The kiss broke as his eyes raked her with a warmth visible even in the dim light. Standing nude before him, all the doubts she held at bay slammed into her like she'd fallen off a horse.

"Dora," he whispered, "love me."

Maybe she worried too much, but his lips covering hers pushed aside her remaining confusion. No promises for tomorrow, only the satisfaction of tonight.

Reluctantly, he released her mouth, and she felt bereft at the loss. Moving from her embrace, he quickly finished unbuttoning his pants, shucking them and tossing the unwanted garment away.

Now he stood naked before her, all male. His manhood protruded, smooth and long and hard. The moonlight streaming through the window cast an iridescent glow about him.

With a cry, she reached out and touched his face, her hand caressing his cheek and pulling him toward her. "I want you, Jesse."

His lips covered hers and she found herself being laid gently down. The mattress sagged when he joined her on the bed, and she ached with the need for Jesse.

With his mouth, he trailed down her chest until he reached her breasts, and his mouth closed over her nipple. Jesse laving the bud, she gripped his head, her breathing harsh.

Slowly his hands skimmed her body, sending shivers through her while his fingers delved into the soft curls that covered her femininity. When he touched her, she jerked at the unexpected jolt of pleasure that rippled through her. Oh how she wanted him desperately, yet she was afraid.

"I'm going to tease you until you beg me to stop," he gasped, breathing hard to fill his lungs.

A moan escaped her, the sound loud and voracious in the darkened room as she arched against his hand, gripping the sheets against the raging need building with his caresses.

"Jesse!" she cried as she tensed, trying to hold on to the sweeping pleasure that ascended on her as she disintegrated beneath his hand.

For a moment, she lay still, her breathing shallow and fast, her eyes closed while she slowly collected herself. Until a thoroughly aroused Jesse, lying beside her, caught her attention.

When she opened her eyes, she gazed at him, his eyes dark, hungry, and so beautiful, she had to resist the urge to kiss each one.

Why now? Why with Jesse when she didn't want to love him, didn't want these emotions. But there was no denying he made her experience life. Every day, he made her laugh and sometimes made her cry, but most of all, he made her feel alive. And she could not deny she loved him.

Her hand slid past his waist, teasing him, getting just close enough to brush her hand across the tip of his manhood. Watching him, anticipation rippled across his face.

"Now who will be doing the begging?"

Finally, she wrapped her hand around his rock-hard shaft. Gently she slid her palm along the top and grasped her fingers around him and stroked the hot, smooth length of him, gripping him until he grabbed her hand.

Rolling himself on top of her, he caught and held both her hands above her head.

When her hands could not do the job, she writhed beneath him, teasing him with her body.

He slid his body down her breasts, her thighs, still holding her hands captive in his own.

"Enough, Dora," he whispered, his husky voice sending tremors down her spine. "It's past time for me to feel you wrapped around me."

His knees nudged open her thighs, his hands gripped her waist as he brought her hips up to meet him and he entered her in a single thrust.

A moan escaped her, the sound loud in the small room as he pushed into her welcoming body.

"Jesse," she cried, unable to contain the passion their bodies created.

"Do you want me to stop?" he asked, staring at her, his gaze hard and unwavering.

"Not until I die," she said as she rose to meet each thrust.

Passion gripped her as he delved into her rhythmically, filling her, melding her to him while she clutched him, relishing in the slide of his flesh against hers.

With every recurring thrust, his moans filled someplace deep within her heart that had been empty for so very long. Sweat glistened on his brow, and Dora reached up to caress his face with her hand.

Opening his eyes, he stared at her, filling her soul as well as her body with sweetness, with a contentment that had long been denied. A pleasure that, even now, was rushing toward her, unstoppable.

As her body went rigid, spasms of desire surrounding Jesse, Dora moaned with satisfaction. Cascading shivers of delight left her clinging to Jesse while he reached his own climax, shuddering, gripping her, as he found his gratification.

Dora breathed deeply the musky scent of Jesse and pressed her lips to the inside of his neck between gasps for air. Completely spent, she lay relaxed, sated, and more confused than ever by the sensations Jesse seemed to generate.

Jesse's breathing was fast and shallow as he leaned against her. For several minutes, they held onto each other, their pulses slowly returning to normal.

"Damn, Dora," he said softly. "How in the hell can a man top that?"

Amazed their thoughts were so closely related, she laughed. Yet a part of her heart began to crack. No matter what, they could never be together forever.

CHAPTER FORTY-TWO

The next morning, she sat in the lawyer's office, knowing this was necessary.

"Mrs. Tennyson, are you certain you want to give this land to these children?"

"Yes," she said, realizing she could never take their home from them after everything they'd lost. This would leave her with nothing. No home, no man, no children, no money, absolutely nothing. But determined, she would survive.

She would persevere, though at this moment, her heart was splintered, aching with the loss of Jesse.

Before the sun rose, she slipped out the hotel room and knew what needed to be done. As much as she loved Jesse, he wanted a son and daughter of his own and she could never give him babies, no matter how much her infertility broke her. She would sacrifice their love to make certain he had the family he desired.

So this morning before he awoke, she packed, dressed, and when she closed the door, it was the hardest thing she'd ever done in her life.

Hurrying down the street, she found a cafe and sat contemplating her next move, waiting for the lawyer's office to open. These last few weeks she felt more alive than ever before. Jesse awakened the woman in her unlike anything she'd ever experienced, and now she would walk away from the man who made her the happiest.

"How long will it take you to draw up the papers?" she asked, coming back to the present. "Sometime today, Jesse Moore will be headed to Dallas to pick up the children. I'd like for him to receive the paperwork before he leaves."

The lawyer nodded and stared at her quizzically trying to figure her out. "You know, there are not many women who would hand over land to their husband's mistress's kids."

With a nod, she said, "Yes, but it's not their fault their father was worthless and it's not their fault that their mother was deceived. Besides, this is their home."

With a sigh, the man shook his head. "This should be delivered to his hotel in the next hour. I'll file the necessary documents with the state."

Dora stood, knowing she should get on the road to Zenith and leave Austin before Jesse realized she was gone. So he wouldn't try to talk her out of leaving, she needed to put as many miles as possible between them.

Maybe he wouldn't regret marrying her today, but sooner or later, he would be disappointed, and she couldn't do that to him.

"Thank you," she said, reaching out and shaking his hand. Quickly, she paid him and walked out the door.

Now Grace, Ella, and Ben would continue to live in the home they were used to. She had five hundred dollars between her and desperation. As a child, she never worried about money or eating or anything, but as a grown woman, her husband left her destitute.

Just when she thought she would recover her losses, she learned someone needed them more than she did.

When she walked into the bright sunlight, she took a deep

breath and sighed. It was done. She climbed onto her horse's back and spurred him down the road to Zenith.

Leo was really dead this time. Grace, Ella, and Ben were taken care of, hopefully, for life. Jesse had captured her heart. But she rode out of town a broken woman, alone.

CHAPTER FORTY-THREE

*J*esse sat in the hotel room waiting, hoping she would return, knowing she was gone. Had last night not meant anything? Couldn't she see he had fallen in love with her? And he thought she was falling in love with him, but this morning his world came crashing down.

All morning, he delayed his departure, praying she would come back. But her saddlebags, everything she owned, had disappeared.

With a sigh, he finished packing his clothes. Time to give up and start the journey to Dallas. Though he couldn't believe he had to return without Dora. For some reason, he believed after they picked up the children, they would find a judge and get married.

Last night he didn't want to talk about their situation. Last night had been about the two of them. Today, he planned on asking her to marry him. But she was gone.

Somewhere along the trail, he fell in love with Dora. Yes, he wanted a family of his own, but he wanted Dora more. He wanted this strong vibrant woman next to him regardless of whether or not she had his babies.

Maybe it was meant to be. Maybe he was not supposed to have his own kids but raise his sister's. And he loved those kids dearly and that would be all right, but he still loved and wanted Dora.

Dora tried to act like she didn't like children. Could that have been her way of protecting her heart? He'd heard and seen her with Ella, and if that wasn't love, then he didn't have a clue about the emotion. To keep from becoming too attached, she put up a wall, a mechanism to protect herself.

A knock sounded on the door as he finished stuffing his saddle bags.

Walking to the door, he opened the entrance to a man in a suit. "Are you Jesse Moore?"

"Yes," he said.

"May I come in?"

"I'm getting ready to leave," he said, thinking he wanted to get on the road.

"Won't take but a moment. It's in regards to Dora Tennyson," he said.

For a second, his breath stopped as fear gripped Jesse and he swung the door wide. "Come in. Is she all right?"

The man stepped inside and gazed at him quizzically. "Seemed fine when she left my office this morning."

He sank in a chair at the table and opened an envelope. "I'm sorry, I should introduce myself. Thomas Ryan, attorney at law. Mrs. Tennyson came by and asked me to draw up a document handing over the land owned by her dead husband to Grace, Ella, and Ben Tennyson."

Shock reverberated through Jesse. She'd given the children their home back. With surprise, he realized what that meant. She had nothing. No money. No property, nothing.

"As their guardian - you are their guardian, right?"

"Yes," he said, plopping down across from the man.

"I need you to sign here showing upon their eighteenth

birthday they will receive the property. The land cannot be sold and she hopes they live out their childhood there," he said.

For three kids who were not hers, but rather her husband's, she was being generous. Though Grace he knew was included because she wanted to be fair.

"Where do I sign," Jesse said, thinking if this was what Dora wanted, he would certainly fulfill her wishes. Though he wished she would be by his side.

"Right here." The lawyer pointed.

Quickly, he signed.

"This paperwork will be filed with the state and the county," he said, rising. "Mr. Moore, Mrs. Tennyson was extremely generous. In all my years, I have never known a woman who wanted to make certain her husband's illegitimate children were taken care of."

The word *illegitimate* went all over Jesse. "Dora adored them as much as my sister loved her children. Just like my sister, she was a victim of Leo Tennyson. Since their parents are gone, she needed to know they were well cared for and had a place to live."

"That's what she said," the man said, standing. "Oh, and there's one more thing. Here's a letter she asked me to give you."

With shock, Jesse reached out and took the envelope with Dora's handwriting.

The man walked out. "Good luck, Mr. Moore."

"Thank you," Jesse said as he closed the door behind him and ripped open the paper.

Dearest Jesse,

Last night was the happiest night of my life, so don't think my leaving means I don't love you. Because I do. Unfortunately, life has dealt me something I cannot change. As much as I would love to bear your children, I can't. For some reason, God made me barren and you want a son who looks like you to carry on your name and a little girl.

Because I love you so very much and I want you to be happy, I've left Austin for good. Please find some wonderful woman who will love your sister's children and give you the babies you want. Have a wonderful life and know I will think of you daily with fondness and love.

Be happy,
Dora

Tears welled up in his eyes as his chest ached with the loss. Yes, he wanted a family, but more than anything, he wanted Dora. With a sigh, he folded the letter and placed the missive in his pocket.

For his happiness, she was putting his needs above her own and giving him the chance for children. Only that no longer mattered. If he had Dora and his nieces and nephew, what more could a man want?

Sadness overwhelmed him as he walked out of the hotel. Time to return to his responsibilities. Yet, his heart wanted him to find Dora and convince her that they were meant to be together with or without children.

CHAPTER FORTY-FOUR

Two days later, Jesse rode into the yard of his aunt Matilda's home. The kids came running out the door like they thought they would never see him again.

"Uncle Jesse," Ella cried, wrapping her arms around his legs, hugging him so tightly, his throat clogged with tears.

Even Grace came bounding down the steps to wrap her arm around his waist. "We're so glad you came back."

"Didn't you believe me when I said I would return for you?"

A sheepish expression crossed her face. "Yes and no. Everyone seems to leave."

Her words made his chest ache because it seemed true. Soon he would need to tell the children their father was dead. No wonder the child felt that way.

"Grace, unless something happens to me, I'll always be here for you. There's something we need to talk about," he said, wanting to tell them about their father.

"Where's Dora?" Ella asked looking around. "Didn't she come back with you? Is she dead?"

The little girl began to cry. "No, not Dora."

Grace glanced up at him with tears in her eyes. "She died?"

Stunned at their response, especially Grace, he stared at the girls.

"No, Dora is not dead," he said. "We need to sit and talk."

Taking both girls by the hand, he started toward the house. His aunt stood in the door, watching the reunion, holding Ben. "Welcome back, Jesse. These kids missed you."

"And I missed them. Were they good?"

"Of course," his aunt replied.

Ben smiled at him and held out his arms. Jesse took him and hugged the little boy, his heart overflowing with love for the child. "Momma?"

Every time he asked, Jesse didn't know what to say.

"Ben means Dora," Grace said.

Walking inside the house, he sat the toddler on his feet, and took his hand as they went into the parlor. As he sat on the sofa, he knew this would not be an easy conversation. What good news could he tell them except they were now landholders? That Dora had given up the land for them.

"Why do you look sad?" Grace said. "You said Dora was all right."

"Yes, she is. But your father was killed by a woman in Austin."

Grace's hands flew to her face and Ella gazed at him quizzically like she didn't believe someone would harm Leo.

"Why would she do that?" Ella asked. "Why would she shoot Papa?"

That he didn't want to explain for many years. "The lady was mad at your papa," he said.

"Did she hurt Dora?" Grace asked.

For a kid who didn't act like she cared much for Dora, she certainly garnered her attention today.

"No, in fact, she saved Dora's life," he said, hoping they didn't ask how.

Grace sat back looking stunned, her eyes welling with tears. "Now we have no parents. What are we going to do?"

Jesse reached over and laid his hand on her arm. "You've got me. Like I told you, I'm not going anywhere. We're going to go back to the house and plant some crops. I'll work on cabinets and do whatever I can to bring in a little money. You guys are my family and I love you. This is what your mother wanted, and I want as well."

Ella started to cry. "I want Dora to be our new momma."

"So do I," Jesse said, not hiding his disappointment.

"Why did she leave?" Grace asked. "Why didn't she stay with you? Did you fight?"

These girls didn't exactly make it easy on a guy. Aunt Matilda glanced at him, her brows raised. They were all curious as to why Dora deserted him. How much could he tell them without going too far?

"Dora left because she didn't think we wanted her. She was trying to be nice and give me the chance to find someone better than her. That's not what I wanted. If I could find her, I would tell her I love her, and yes, I want her badly."

"We should go after her," Grace said.

How should he react? Of course, he wanted to go after her, but he hadn't expected the kids to be so upset at Dora not being with him. For them to say they wanted her to be their mother surprised him.

"But I don't know where she lives," he said.

"Zenith," Grace said. "She told me she lived in Zenith."

How could this child have more information about the woman he loved than he did? For over a day, he'd been racking his brain to remember the town she lived in.

"Let's go find her and tell her we want her to be our new mother and for her to be your wife," Grace said.

Strange how this was coming from the child who had given Dora the most grief.

"Are you certain?" he asked.

"Yes," Grace said. "Are you certain you want to marry her?"

"Yes," he said in frustration, thinking he had planned on asking her the day she left.

Grace grinned. "One request if you get married."

"What?" he said, thinking these children gave him direction that he needed.

"I don't want to listen to the two of you arguing. Promise us we won't hear screaming and yelling."

The child's words made him sad. How bad was his sister's marriage to Leo if their kids heard them fighting?

"Yeah," Ella said. "No hitting either."

Dear God, if Leo wasn't dead, he would be after this conversation.

"It's a promise. No screaming. No hitting," he said.

"Let's go get our new momma," Ella said, jumping up from the couch where she'd been sitting.

His aunt Matilda held up her hands. "Wait, no one has eaten or bathed and the time is late. Why don't you stay the night and leave first thing in the morning?"

Jesse couldn't agree more, though he was anxious to reach Zenith. Poor Dora had no idea what kind of trouble was headed her way. Because if they found her, she would have three children and a man all trying to convince her to marry him. To join and become an instant family.

Ben jumped up and down and said, "Momma, momma, momma."

How did the toddler understand what they were talking about?

CHAPTER FORTY-FIVE

Dora realized that soon she would have to return to hunting for criminals, but she needed some rest. Leaving Jesse seemed to have drained her and she felt broken.

Last night she stayed in a hotel, but later today she planned on riding out to visit Ruby. In the last days of her friend's pregnancy, she wanted to make certain the woman was fine and talk to her about this business.

It was more stressful than she thought possible, but she didn't know if that was because she knew Leo or if it would always be this way.

This morning, she was on her way to the dress shop to see Meg and say hello. She also needed to visit Quinlan and check on her. This town was her backbone and if she had money, she would never leave, but with her giving the land away, that was impossible.

The bell rang above the door as she entered, and Annabelle came from the back. "Oh my, look who is back from her first bounty hunting trip."

The woman ran to Dora and gave her a hug. "It's so great to see you. Did you catch him?"

With a laugh, Dora nodded. "Yes, I'm a widow once again."

"Please tell me you didn't kill him."

A sigh escaped Dora. "No, a woman he was courting shot him to protect me. He was going to shoot me in the back."

"Oh, dear," Annabelle said. "So glad you're safe. What a scoundrel."

"How's everyone? Meg, did she have her baby? And Ruby, is she doing all right?"

Annabelle grinned and motioned Dora over to a crib in the kitchen. "Today, I'm watching the shop and the baby, letting Meg rest. Isn't he the sweetest newborn?"

Dora glanced in the tiny wooden bed and it was all she could do to keep the tears at bay. This was what she wanted so badly with Jesse, but not possible. "He's so precious."

"Meg is resting and Deke is making certain Ruby takes it easy. She's due any day now."

"How exciting," Dora said. "Later today, I plan on going out to see Ruby."

The tinkle of the bell over the door alerted them there were customers. Jesse's voice reached out and tugged at her heart.

"Are you sure you saw her come in here?"

"Momma," Ben called out.

The words wrenched inside her chest and she looked for an escape route. Jesse and the children had followed her and all she wanted to do was scurry out the back door to keep from facing him.

The man understood her situation, so why was he here? Tears she'd dammed up erupted and ran down her face as she gazed at the sleeping baby. For Jesse's sake, she must run.

"Can I help you," Annabelle asked as she went to greet the new arrivals.

With tears flowing down her cheeks, Dora opened the back

door of the shop and ran outside. She had to hide. She had to leave before he completely devastated her.

Running behind the buildings, she rounded the corner and came face to face with the man she was hiding from.

"Damn, Dora, you are the stubbornest, most defiant woman I've ever met. Why are you running from me?"

The two of them stood in the alley and she stared at the man she loved. Why wouldn't he leave her alone and let her heart heal? "You know why. I'm trying to do the right thing. I'm walking away so you can have your dream."

Her chest ached with pain and she so wanted to throw her arms around him, but that would be crazy.

"I don't say this very often, but I'm going to. Shut up and listen to me."

He took a deep breath. "All that matters is I love you so much. The thought of not seeing your beautiful, smiling face each morning when I wake up and kissing you before I go to sleep at night...I need you.

"Nothing else has meaning if you're not by my side. All I want is for you to be my wife, my partner, and yes, the mother to the three children I'm going to raise. We're a family and I don't need anyone else but you."

Eventually he would hate her for what she couldn't give him. Just like Leo hated her and went in search of another life.

"But I can't give you what—"

"Stop," he took her in his arms. "That doesn't matter to me. All that matters is that I love you."

His hand reached out and wiped the tears from her face and she could feel her once strong insides turning to mush.

"Marry me. I promise I will never steal from you. I'll never marry another woman and I'll be by your side loving you. Your giving of the land was beyond generous, but there's something more those kids need. They need you. I need you."

She bit her lip, so wanting to tell him yes, but fear held her in its grip. "Oh, Jesse, I want to say yes, but I'm not certain the children really want me as their mother."

"Are you kidding me. When I reached Dallas, they were insistent we come find you. Three kids were mad I let you get away. Grace and Ella wanted to leave at that moment. And Ben kept walking around saying momma," he said. "But more than anything, I need you. Together, they need us."

They wanted her as their mother? Both Grace and Ella? Filled with more love than she could contain, tears streamed down her cheeks.

"Yes," she said. "As long as you understand, I can't give you what you want."

"You're giving me everything I want. Your love and being by my side every day for as long as I live."

His lips covered hers and he sealed the deal with a kiss. The sound of children's voices reached her ears.

"Ewww, they're kissing," Ella said.

"That's good," Grace told her. "That means they're in love."

When they broke apart, she smiled at Jesse and gazed at the three of them waiting for her answer. Her instant family.

"Momma, please say yes to Daddy. We want you to come home with us," Grace said.

Tears welled in Dora's eyes. Grace, the stubborn one, called her momma. "You're certain?"

"Yes," Grace said.

"Yes," Ella said.

Ben held out his arms and said, "Momma."

Unable to resist, she reached down and picked him up and he gave her a slobbery kiss that melted her chest.

This was so right, how could she say no? Glancing at Jesse, the man she loved with all her heart, she said, "Yes, I'll marry you."

The girls jumped up and down and Ella took her hand. "Grace and I planned the wedding while you were gone with Uncle Jesse. You should get married at home out in the sunshine."

"Sounds like a wonderful idea, Ella."

"Come on," Jesse said, "let's head home. We have a wedding to finish planning."

The baby in her arms, Jesse took her hand and the girls followed them toward their wagon. Dora's heart overflowed with love. In searching for her dead husband, she found a man she loved and a ready-made family of her own. Now her life was complete.

CHAPTER FORTY-SIX

*O*ne Year Later

The mid-wife glanced at her. "One more push and the baby will be here."

Jesse lifted his wife's back helping to give her more strength. "Come on, honey, you can do this. This has been your dream."

Exhausted, Dora gave one last huge push, putting all her remaining energy behind this final effort and suddenly she felt the infant leave her body.

The woman laughed as she wiped the child's face clean of the mucus and a healthy cry ensued.

"A son," the woman said, holding up the child for Dora and Jesse to see.

Tears ran down Dora's cheeks and even Jesse was crying.

"I never believed this would happen," Dora cried.

The mid-wife cut the umbilical cord, wrapped the baby in a blanket and handed him to Dora. She gazed down at her son and then at Jesse. "He's a miracle child."

Jesse kissed his wife and stared at their son. "No, honey, he's the product of love. Maybe the reason you never had children before was because there was no love. This time, there is so much love in this home, he was bound to come along."

Dora knew the words he said were true. In all her years, she could not remember being this happy. And this child made them complete. The baby opened his eyes and gazed at his parents.

"Welcome, son. You are so wanted and loved," Dora whispered, gazing at the marvel in her arms.

Outside the bedroom, they could hear the children's voices. They had been ordered to remain there until Jesse opened the door. But her children probably had their ears pressed to the door listening and would know the baby had arrived. "Unless you want a mutiny, you need to let them in."

Placing his lips against her mouth, he gave her a quick kiss. "Do you know how much I love you?"

"As much as I love you."

He grinned, kissed the baby's forehead, and warned him. "Better get tough fast, little man. You've got two older sisters and a brother who are dying to meet you."

When Jesse stepped away from the bed and outside the door, she heard him giving instructions to their children. "Remember, the baby just arrived and your mother is feeling tired. Three minutes to say hello and then bed time."

"Is momma all right?" Grace asked.

The child worried if she got a cold, probably because of the death of her own mother and her father. The girl was growing into a beautiful young lady and had become her biggest helper especially during the unexpected pregnancy.

"She's tired, but she's fine," Jesse assured her.

As Jesse cracked the door open, the three of them ran into the room. Ben had grown into a tenacious little boy and pushed his sisters out of the way as he rushed to her side. "Momma, is it a boy?"

"Yes, son, the baby is a boy. A little brother for you," she said, holding the child so Ben saw him.

"Yeah, now it's two and two," he said.

Not that Ben was an underdog. He managed to control his sisters and keep them in line.

Each child was unique in their own way and Ben was all boy. Needing to touch him, she reached out and ruffled his hair and realized how much she loved her life.

Ella came to the bed and she gazed at her and the baby. "Do you still love us?"

The question stunned her, considering she spent nine months telling them this didn't change her feelings for them. "More than ever. Because you were my children first and led me to Jesse. Without the three of you, I wouldn't have a family. Now we're just a family of six, not five."

Ella leaned over and kissed her on the cheek. "He's so tiny."

Grace stood off to the side as she always did, observing and taking everything in. Instinctively knowing how nervous she could become, Dora took her hand. "Grace, you are our oldest, and you are each special to your father and me. We love all of you and now there's a new member of our family."

"What's his name?" she asked.

"We haven't decided yet," Dora told her. "What do you suggest?"

"Jesse, after Papa," she said.

Dora squeezed her hand. "I like that idea. We'll talk about it."

Jesse wrapped them in his arms. "All right, your mother needs to rest. Time you younglings went to bed."

Dora blew them all a kiss and watched as her husband ushered them out the door. After shooing them off to bed, Jesse returned to her and leaned down, watching their son sleep on her chest.

"When I married you, I accepted we would not have children together. And if we never have another one, it won't matter. You're all that matters to me. You are still the love of my life."

Dora's heart overflowed with love. Marrying Jesse had been the best thing she'd ever done. Reaching up, she kissed him while holding their son in her arms. "Dear husband, you make my heart complete," she whispered.

* * *

The Last Historical Lipstick and Lead Book Devious

RACING across the lawn in the darkness, eighteen-year-old Addie King skipped out of washing the supper dishes by disappearing to the outhouse.

Hopefully by the time she returned, her brother and sister would have everything washed and dried. Then she could go back to reading her new favorite book, the *Bumbling Bounty Hunter*.

Tonight, she wanted to finish the story before she went to sleep, so that tomorrow she would give her full attention to her chores.

An owl hooted as she sprinted through the grass. She hated going out at night, but she disliked washing dishes even more. The distant neighing of a horse sent a tremor of unease down her spine. Papa's horses were in the barn and usually quiet.

As she shut the outhouse door behind her, she quickly did her business. Just as she was about to return to the house, she heard a team of horses, their hooves thundering into the yard. Shouting and cursing and gunshots firing off in the air sent a trickle of fright racing down her spine.

"Frank King, show your face," a voice shouted.

Addie glanced between the cracks of the wooden door and saw seven rough looking men with guns and torches had surrounded her home. What could they want?

A shiver of anxiety gripped her. Papa had been talking low to her mother about trouble. Glancing around, she wanted to run to the house, but she would have to run right by the frightening men who blocked her path.

Her father stepped outside with his rifle. Being the most peace-loving man in the county, Papa never carried a gun.

The leader held a burning torch in his hand. The glow from the flames was high enough for her to see his hardened features. Framed by coal back hair, a jagged scar ran down the left side of the leader's face, his beady dark eyes sent a shiver through her.

"The Colonel gave you until last night at midnight to agree to sell your property. The deadline has passed. Are you selling?"

With a gasp, she watched her father raise his rifle in his arms---not pointing the muzzle at anyone but using it almost as a shield. "We're not selling."

In the hellish glow of the torches, she stared at the threatening man, fear paralyzing her. A grin spread across his contorted face like he was delighted her father had refused the man's offer.

"Last chance. The Colonel will give you a thousand dollars for your land."

Defiant, Papa spat on the ground. "We're staying."

A laugh of pure pleasure came from the ugly man's lips. The sound eerie in the flickering light.

"Shoot him," he commanded.

The men raised their guns and fired, their muzzles flashing light. An anguished cry stuck in her throat as her father crumpled to the ground.

Addie covered her mouth to muffle the terror that escaped with her voice.

Screaming, her mother ran from the house, her skirts flowing behind her as she knelt beside her husband. Another round of gunshots and Addie jerked as gunfire felled her mother's body onto her dead husband. Tears streamed down Addie's face.

She wanted to run to her parents, but fear kept her in hiding.

With a sob, she stared at each man and committed his face to memory. They would not get away with murdering her parents.

Then in horror, she watched as the ruthless men began to set fires around the wooden home. At the last moment, they tossed their torches through the windows as the house exploded with smoke and flames.

Oh, how she wanted to race to her brother and sister but knew she would only become another of their victims. Her chest ached with anger and fear and the need to scream her frustration.

"Put those bodies in the house and then lay some arrows around the home. It needs to look like an Indian attack," the scarred man ordered.

With despair, she watched as they tossed her parents' bodies into the flames.

Laughing, the gang rode off into the night. She burst from the outhouse, running to the house, screaming their names.

"James, Sammie," she cried pleading with God to let her save them.

When she tried to enter the house, the flames pushed her back, and she knew. No one could live through that inferno.

Sinking to the ground, a soul wrenching animal cry tore through her body. Everything she had known and loved had been ripped from her life.

The memory of the scar-faced man came to mind. Who was the Colonel? Rage overcame her and while she wanted to scream, fear of them returning kept her silent.

All night she grieved, planning her escape, her revenge.

And she didn't want any of them to know an avenger would soon be on their trail.

At dawn, she noticed the barn was still standing and hurried inside. She found her father's hidden stash of cash and a set of silver pistols in a cabinet. Thank goodness, he hid some money away from the house. She released all the horses, but her own, which she saddled.

As the sun peeked over the horizon, she took one last glance at the smoldering remains of her home. Staring, she dried her tears and placed her hand over her heart. "I swear on my soul that your deaths will be vindicated. I will find the Colonel and his men. They will hang for murdering you."

Filled with anguish, she climbed into the saddle and forced herself to turn her horse away from her old life. Not trusting the law in Harper's Mill, she rode toward Zenith, Texas. She rode toward the Lipstick and Lead Bounty Hunting School and the beginning of her revenge.

Click Here! Coming July 11, 2019

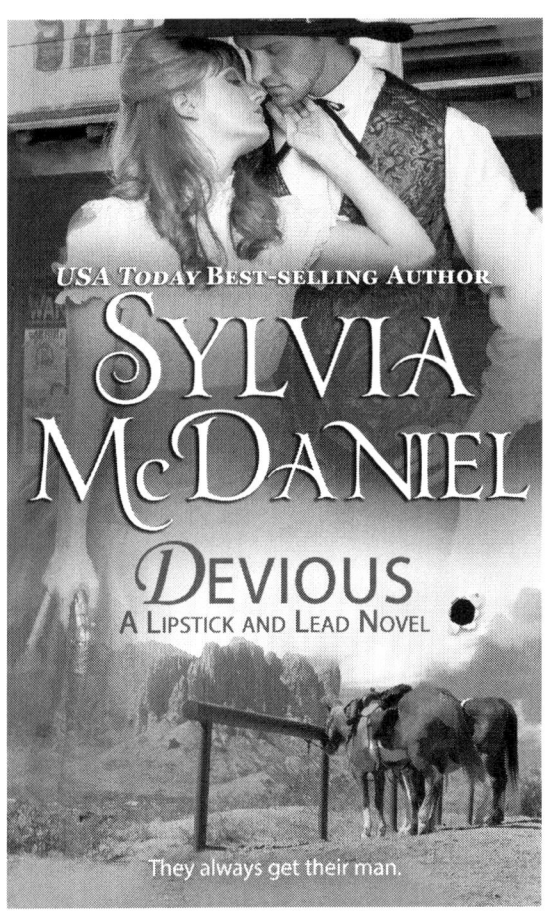

LEAVE A REVIEW

Did you enjoy Defiant? Reviews help authors and are very much appreciated.
Click here to leave a review!

Join the new book alerts here.

Join the Facebook Group and hang out with us!

Psst…don't forget to follow me on Bookbub.

Bounty Hunter Women –They Always Get Their Man.

In 1880 Zenith Texas, the McKenzie sisters, Meg, Annabelle and Ruby find themselves penniless after the death of their father. When the bank threatens foreclosure, the women realize they need a way to support themselves. They have three options; marriage, women's work or… following in their papa's footsteps.

For More Information Click Here!

Lipstick and Lead Video

The Burnett Brides
The Rancher Takes a Bride Book 1

Texas 1874

Rose Severin made her living speaking to the dead. Or at least she pretended to, until she could fulfill her real dream of becoming a famous actress on the New York stage like her mother. But dreams couldn't put a roof over your head or ease the gnawing ache of hunger, and New York was more than a carriage ride from Fort Worth, Texas.

Rose peeked between the curtain separating the two rooms and watched her black manservant, Isaiah, settle tonight's customers. She'd drawn an interesting group. A fairly young woman, a matron, a swanky gentleman, and a cowboy whose burnished hair and rugged good looks certainly caught her attention.

Isaiah stepped behind the curtain and whispered, "Mrs. Florin, the lady who will be sitting next to you, lost her twelve-year-old daughter, Sally, in a carriage accident. She wants to contact Sally and make sure she's all right. The other lady, Miss North, wishes to speak with her brother who was killed in a bank holdup. He was a law-abiding man, just in the wrong place at the wrong time, according to the newspaper."

Isaiah frowned and shook his head. "The gentleman in the brown suit, Mr. Thompson, said very little. The other man, Mr. Burnett, is here because of his brother."

"Burnett. That name sounds familiar." Rose tried to remember where she had heard the name before.

"His mother came in earlier this afternoon. She's the lady who wanted to speak with her missing son. He disappeared during the war and she didn't know if he was dead or alive."

"Yes, I remember her." Rose glanced out the curtain. "What does he want?"

"He wouldn't say."

"I guess we'll find out," she said shaking her head and frowning at Isaiah.

"Are you ready?" Isaiah asked.

Rose brushed back a lock of her dark, wayward curls, checked the bodice of her loose-fitting blouse, and smoothed her skirt. Dressed more like a gypsy than a lady, she took a deep breath and released it slowly. "Madame Desiree is ready."

Isaiah ambled out of the kitchen and turned toward the group of people now gathered around the table. "Let me present Madame Desiree Severin, Voice of the Dead."

Rose swept through the curtain. Holding out her full skirt, she gave a little twirl then curtsied to her audience. "Good evening."

She pulled out a chair and took a seat between the cowboy and Mrs. Florin. She glanced around the table at the four customers who had come to speak with their departed loved ones.

Madame Desiree offered her clients a chance to ease their conscience, say the words they'd meant to say, resolve a disagreement, or for a brief moment feel close to the dead once again.

Whatever reason brought them to her, Rose tried her best to

give them their money's worth, and if it eased their pain, then she'd more than fulfilled her job.

She lowered her head as if praying, then raised her brows, gazing at each person sitting around the table.

"*Alors, commencon.*" She paused dramatically, letting her customers absorb the French words and then repeated them in English. "Let us begin."

With a flick of her wrist, she snapped her fingers at Isaiah, her bracelets jingling. From the back of the room, he turned the knob of the lantern until the light slowly faded and a faint glimmer remained, casting the room in an eerie twilight.

The rough scratch of a match striking flint echoed in the darkness as she lit the mixture of cedar, thyme, rose petals, and vanilla. A cloud of smoky perfume drifted upwards, leaving a faint glow in the metal bowl.

"Close your eyes and hold the hand of your neighbor as I call upon the spirits to heed our summons," she commanded in a French accent that she'd practiced.

Isaiah plunged the room into darkness. Like an invisible bond, nervous tension flowed through the room, weaving a seductive spell over her clients.

A quick glance at the cowboy showed the corner of his mouth lifted in amusement. So, he thought this was entertaining, did he? She lifted his hand, rough callused but warm and strong as he clasped her small hand in his.

He gazed back at her, his eyebrows questioning.

She'd dealt with men like him before. She lifted her chin and turned her gaze to her other customers.

"Many spirits are gathered in the room with us tonight," she whispered. She turned her face toward the heavens and called out loud, "Spirits, come to us. Let us speak with our dear departed ones again."

With practiced ease, Rose quietly slipped her foot out of her backless boot. Her bare foot touched the hardwood floor as she eased it under her chair, until she touched the cool metallic bell. Gripping the handle of the bell between her toes, Rose shook the bell. The clapper clattered against its side three times.

A lady sitting across from Rose jumped. Isaiah silently came in right on cue, stirring the air with a fan in the darkened room. Then the sound of chimes tinkled softly in the night air.

Releasing the cowboy's hand, she clasped her palm to her head, moaning. "Ah...ah, so young. So tragic." She swayed. "A little girl with blond ringlets is coming toward me, wearing a pink pinafore. She says her name is Sar...no, her name is Sally."

A gasp came from the darkness and one of the Women said in a weak voice, "My daughter's name was Sally, but her hair was dark, not blond." Her voice broke on a sob. "Is it Sally? Tell me more about her, please. Is she happy?"

Rose ignored the woman's comment about her daughter's hair. "Sally says to tell you she's with her grandmother."

Rose hesitated and then began to move her lips silently, as if she were speaking. "The two of them miss you and are awaiting your arrival on the other side."

The lady burst into tears. "Thank God, she's not alone. I've been so worried about her."

"Families often are reunited after death." Rose moaned and pulled her handkerchief to her lips.

"I feel the presence of a man who was gunned down. A law-abiding man killed in a holdup."

"My brother," the older woman sitting next to Rose proclaimed.

Rose massaged her temples, moaning. She held up her arms as if seeking help from the sky. "Is his name Robert?"

"Yes," the woman replied, stunned. "How did you know?"

"He told me. He says you shouldn't feel guilty about his death. It was meant to happen. Your grandfather is with him."

"But grandfather is still alive," the woman said, puzzled.

Rose felt a moment of panic. Whoops, she'd guessed wrong

again. The lady's age appeared to be in the mid-forties. Rose had been certain her grandparents were dead. She let out a moan. "I meant your great-grandfather."

"Oh, we never knew him."

The cowboy beside her snickered just loudly enough to be heard. He was going to cause trouble, blast him.

"Oh, oh. The name Burnett comes to mind." She moaned. "Does anyone know someone named Tanner Burnett?"

"That's me," a husky, curt voice from her left replied.

It was the cowboy. Even in the dark, she couldn't help but remember six feet of rugged, tightly muscled man with honey-brown hair set against tanned skin and eyes that looked more dangerous than friendly.

"Are you certain the person you're seeking is dead?"

She could feel his gaze upon her, and the memory of his brown eyes gleaming with determination and purpose almost made her shiver.

"He's been missing for over ten years," he acknowledged.

"I have a vision of him in battle. There's danger all around him."

His fist slammed against the table, causing sparks to fly from the bowl of incense and her patrons to jump in surprise.

"Bullshit!"

"Lady, how far are you going to carry this farce? You can't see my brother."

"*Monsieur!*" she exclaimed, throwing up her hands in disgust. Gripping the bell with her toe, she rang it, signaling the end of the seance.

"The sound of the bell indicates that the spirits have gone," she said between gritted teeth. "You've broken the spell. The spirits have all departed because of your disbelief. Your doubt has scared them away!"

Isaiah lit a lantern, casting an ominous glow on the scene.

A chill ran down Rose's back as she stared into the coldest

pair of dark-brown eyes she'd ever seen. She stood and turned her attention to her other clients. "I'm terribly sorry, but once the spell has been broken, the spirits will not return this night. Thanks to *Monsieur*, our evening has been cut short. That is the way sometimes. Please come back and we will attempt to contact your loved ones once again." She gave him a look that could have plunged daggers into his heart. "Without *Monsieur* Burnett."

He smiled a contemptuous sneer. "Lady, if you can speak to the dead, I can walk on water! All you're interested in is cheating people out of their money!"

"*Monsieur*!" She motioned for Isaiah to usher her other customers out the door. Business had been good, and she didn't need gossip being spread around town about this little scene. "The Trinity River is right up the street, if you'd like to test your faith."

"I don't need to test my faith. People like you do it all the time," he said.

"If you don't believe in speaking with spirits, why are you here?" she asked bluntly, hoping to get rid of him quickly.

"Everyone deserves at least one warning, and here's yours." He stood and moved around the table. "Don't be holding any more Séances."

"This is a free country, is it not?" she said, using her best French intonation.

"Not for cheats."

"I am no cheat."

"Lose the French accent!"

"I cannot! It is where I was born, where I come from," she informed him.

"I'm sure you've been around, but I'd wager you've never seen Paris," he said calmly, his voice a slow drawl of insolence.

"*Espéce de casse-couilles!*" She said in French exactly what she was thinking. The man was certainly a pain.

"Cut the parlee-voo, lady. I don't believe a word of it."

"You should. I'm calling you, Mr. Burnett, every despicable word I know," she practically shouted at him, enraged at his intrusion in her cozy business.

"Call me anything you want, but I'm warning you. Shut down your séance parlor. You picked the wrong person to try to con, and you're not going to get away with it."

"And just who is this person I supposedly tried to con?" she asked.

"My mother, Eugenia Burnett."

"Ah ha!" Stepping in front of him, she stood within inches of this handsome yet foreboding man. The scent of masculinity drifted to her nose, a clean smell of virile male.

"And if your mother wishes to learn more about your brother? Is this not her choice?"

"My mother misses my brother, and I'll not have you taking advantage of her. This is the only time I'm going to tell you. Leave my mother alone, or I'm going to shut down your parlor."

"*Monsieur!* If you don't want your mother searching for your brother, then you must talk to her. Not I!" She took a step back, letting her gaze travel the length of his person. "Besides, I see no badge. You do not have the authority to threaten me, or shut me down."

He smiled, his full lips pouty, and took a step closer to her. His hand reached out, the tip of his finger gently tracing her chin, his rough skin sliding against hers. His touch left her oddly unsettled. She tried to swallow the lump that filled her throat.

Now was not the time for her long-denied body to suddenly take notice of a man. She needed this town, needed this job.

She didn't need a gun-toting, overprotective mama's boy, who looked like sin in a nicely bundled package.

"I'll shut you down in a heartbeat," he said, low enough only to reach her ears. "My little brother, Tucker, is the marshal."

Picking up his hat, he strolled out the door, his gun slung low around his hips, his pants snug against his backside.

Rose watched him walk through the door and wanted to scream. Though they had gotten off to a slow start, business was just beginning to increase and the thought of having to pick up and start over again left her furious.

No damn cowboy with a connection to the local law was going to run her out of town!

Download Now!

Also By Sylvia McDaniel
Western Historicals
A Hero's Heart
Second Chance Cowboy
Ethan

American Brides
**Katie: Bride of Virginia

Angel Creek Christmas Brides
**Charity
**Ginger
**Minne
**Cora

Bad Girls of the West
Scandalous Sadie
Ravenous Rose
Tempting Tessa
Nellie's Redemption

The Burnett Brides Series
The Rancher Takes A Bride
The Outlaw Takes A Bride
The Marshal Takes A Bride
The Christmas Bride
Boxed Set

Lipstick and Lead Series
Desperate
Deadly
Dangerous

ALSO BY

Daring
**Determined
Deceived
Defiant
Devious
Lipstick and Lead Box Set Books 1-4
Lipstick and Lead Box Set Books 5-9
Lipstick and Lead Box Set Books 1-9
**Quinlan's Quest

Mail Order Bride Tales
**A Brother's Betrayal
**Pearl
**Ace's Bride

Scandalous Suffragettes of the West
**Abigail
Bella
Mistletoe Scandal

Southern Historical Romance
A Scarlet Bride

The Cuvier Women
Wronged
Betrayed
Beguiled
Boxed Set

The Debutante's of Durango
The Debutante's Scandal
The Debutante's Gamble
The Debutante's Revenge
The Debutante's Santa

** Denotes a sweet book.

Want to learn about my new releases before anyone else? Sign up for my New Book Alert and receive a complimentary book.

USA Today Best-selling author, Sylvia McDaniel obviously has too much time on her hands. With over seventy western historical and contemporary romance novels, she spends most days torturing her characters. Bad boys deserve punishment and even good girls get into trouble. Always looking for the next plot twist, she's known for her sweet, funny, family-oriented romances.

Married to her best friend for over twenty-five years, they recently moved to the state of Colorado where they like to hike, and enjoy the beauty of the forest behind their home with their spoiled dachshund Zeus and puppy Bailey. (He has his own column in her newsletter.)

Their grown son, still lives in Texas. An avid football watcher, she loves the Broncos and the Cowboys, especially when they're winning.

www.SylviaMcDaniel.com
Sylvia@SylviaMcDaniel.com
The End!

Manufactured by Amazon.ca
Bolton, ON

37864034R00125